When Eyes Meet
By Michelle Rider

When Eyes Meet

Michelle Rider

Published by Michelle Rider, 2023.

WHEN EYES MEET

First edition. February 7, 2023.

ISBN: 979-8215402542

Written by Michelle Rider.

Table of Contents

To anyone who was picked on in high school or anywhere else...

We are stronger because of it.

You never look good trying to make someone else look bad.

Be kind.

Chapter 1
Ali

Fuck. My. Life.

This cannot be happening. This is the definition of a nightmare.

"So, I will be drawing names and genres out of a hat to determine who will work together on the final. We have discussed the importance of workshopping, but I really think this project will help you understand exactly what I mean," Professor Marshall says in his deep timber.

There are only twenty of us in the writing seminar class, and we all write in varying genres. Mine is mystery. I love the thrill of coming up with motives and making people guess what is going to happen. I can let my imagination run wild and create any number of scenarios.

But I work alone. Every time we have had to share our work this term for feedback from our peers was terrifying. I am one of those people who doesn't mesh well with others. People always have an agenda, and sometimes it's difficult to figure out. I don't trust easily. I never have.

I glance around at the other faces in my class and cringe at the thought of who will torture me for this project. Everyone seems nice enough, but my stomach churns violently at the thought of exposing my creativity.

A bright pair of blue eyes stare back at me, and I immediately blush.

Cole Buchanan. The most gorgeous guy I have seen during my time here at South Bane University. He is one of those guys who is always smiling. I noticed him for the first time during my freshman year, but this is the first class we had together. I had no idea he was even in the same writing program. I would die if I were paired with him. There is no way I would be able to speak around him, let alone let the creative juices flow.

I force my eyes forward, watching in horror as Professor Marshall writes our names on little pieces of paper and puts them into a hat. When he said he would draw names from a hat, I didn't realize he was being literal. Who does that anymore? It is so old-fashioned.

Each name that is read elicits a cringe as I not so patiently wait for my fate. The mystery writer in me feels like this may be how my characters feel as they wait to find out if they are the murderer or not.

Five pairings down. Halfway there.

Each second that passes brings with it a rush of nausea. I know that nothing good will come from this entire scenario.

I don't know whether I want to hear my name or not. It would be great to just get it over with, but I appreciate freedom more and more the longer I go without being called.

"Ali Ewing. Ah, our mystery queen! Who will be your partner?" Marshall says cheerily, making me want to throat-punch him.

Just say the damn name! Just tell me who I have to suffer with for the next few weeks.

"Cole Buchanan. Wonderful! I think this is a great pairing!"

Is it possible to feel your blood rushing to your face? Like every single red blood cell in my body just jumped on the expressway to my cheeks. The heat of embarrassment floods my senses as I fight the urge to vomit.

"And what genre will you be writing?" Marshall says with way too much enthusiasm.

Anything but romance. Anything but romance. Anything but romance! I won't be able to handle it.

"Romance!"

As I said before.

Fuck. My. Life.

After giving us the ridiculous rules for his project, Marshall dismisses us early so that we have a chance to meet with our new partners to figure out the details of working together.

We have one month to complete the assignment. We have to write one scene, no more than two thousand words. For those of us who are writing romance, the heat level of the scene is completely up to us. It can be as closed-door or detailed as we want it, but we have to hit the main components of the genre.

As my classmates pack up their things, I debate running up to Marshall and begging for a different genre or different partner. I'm sure Cole is nice, but we are opposites in everything. He is popular, but I'm not. He's gorgeous, I'm plain. He's open and outgoing, or at least that's how he seems, and I'm the definition of an introvert.

After a few moments of me waiting to wake up from this awful dream that I seem to be having, I feel his presence next to me. I check my body to make sure I have clothes on, worried that this may actually be that dream where I am naked in front of everyone. The smooth cotton of my leggings and hoodie gives me a minuscule bit of relief, but not much. I squeeze my eyes closed in one final desperate attempt to make this not be my reality, but a light tap on my shoulder tells me that I am, in fact, about to embark on what will likely be the most humiliating experience of my life.

"Ali," Cole says. Why does his smooth voice make my name sound so amazing?

Stealing myself, I turn and meet his eyes.

He is wearing a soft smile, his bright white teeth gleaming so brightly that I swear one of those little flashes of light appears in the corner like you see in movies.

"Hi, Cole," I say. Of course, my voice squeaks. Of course.

I try to busy myself with packing my bag, needing to do something so I don't just stare at him awkwardly. Unfortunately, I only had one notebook and pen out, so it takes me all of five seconds.

I stand and grab my bag before I turn to face him.

I have seen him many times around campus and in class, but this is the closest I have ever been to him. The top of my head barely reaches his shoulders, making my eyes the perfect height to stare at the firm muscles of his chest. He is wearing a worn, faded pair of jeans paired with a tight, grey Henley. His arms are thick and probably strong enough to snap me in two if he wanted. I force my gaze on his face and take in his soft smile. There is what appears to be a few days' worth of scruff on his square jaw. But what really gets me is the softness of his eyes.

That old saying that the eyes are the window to the soul comes to mind, and it puts me at ease. I know looks can be deceiving and all, but I don't get the impression that Cole has one mean bone in his body.

He holds his hand out to me. "It's nice to finally meet you, Ali. I'm really looking forward to working with you."

I discretely wipe my palm on my pants before placing my hand in his. The last thing I want to do is get my sweat on his perfect skin.

"Hh… hi. It's nice to meet you, too."

Wait. Did he say finally?

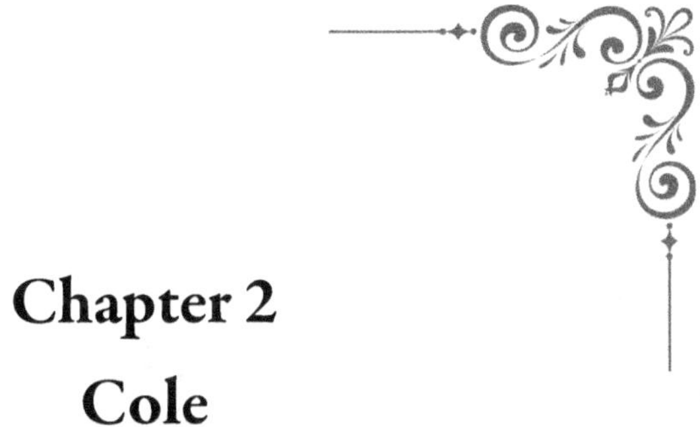

Chapter 2
Cole

The second I hear my name I want to pump my fist in the air.

Ali Ewing.

The most adorably beautiful person, inside and out. Not that I know her, or anything. She's one of those people you can tell is just about perfect. I have wanted to approach her for about a year now, but every time I build up the nerve, she disappears. She is skittish, that's for sure. I never see her with other people. She keeps to herself. But I have found out as much as I can from asking around. One of the benefits of having a lot of friends is that I can get information quickly. That and the fact that a buddy of mine dates her freshman-year roommate, Laura.

From what I heard she lives alone in an apartment not far from campus. She is a junior, like me, and in the same writing program. Laura said she is very quiet but sweet. She loves to read (like most writers I know), and she spends a lot of her time doing research for whatever she is writing at the time. Laura said she asked Ali to room with her again last year, but Ali said she wanted to move off campus. They still get together for lunch every once in a while, and Laura speaks to her pretty regularly.

I managed to get Ali's number from Laura, but not before Laura threatened to cut my balls off with a spoon if I ever hurt her. I still shiver thinking about the picture she painted with the details of how she would do it. Not something any guy ever wants to imagine for his manhood.

"So, do you want to go to the library and talk about our scene?" I ask her.

She hasn't stopped blushing since I approached her. I can tell she is nervous, and that is the last thing I want.

She nods and turns toward the front of the room. I walk behind her, trying like hell not to notice her round ass and the way her hips sway back and forth when she walks. I have known many girls through the frat house who try their hardest and failed to walk seductively, and here is Ali doing it without even trying. She is so alluring, and she has no idea.

The library is only a short walk from the English building, but I use the time to try and get to know her.

"So, what's your favorite mystery novel?" I ask.

Her eyes widen. "I can't pick just one! That would be blasphemous!"

I laugh at her outburst, and she blushes, again. "I'm not laughing at you, Ali. I would have said the same thing if someone asked me to pick my favorite sci-fi. Just trying to break the ice."

She giggles. "Sorry. Guess I snapped a tad." Her voice goes back to the quiet, melodic tone I am used to hearing from the infrequent times she actually speaks in class.

"It's all good," I say, nudging her with my shoulder.

I wait, hoping that I just didn't cross a line by touching her, and am pleasantly surprised when she bumps me back.

"I just think that every book has its own virtues, you know? I may love one for the characters, and another for the intensity. Every single one is different in their own way. I wouldn't be able to pick one over another any easier than I could choose between my guinea pigs."

"You have guinea pigs?" I ask and her face flushes as she nods. "I love guinea pigs! I always wanted to get one, but the guys at the house would terrorize them for sure."

"You don't seem like the kind of guy who would like them," she says softly.

"What kind of guy do I seem like?" I ask, wanting to know what she thinks of me.

"Uh, well... I guess you seem more like a sports guy, like someone who likes to party."

"Because I live in the frat house?"

She nods.

"You know why I joined the fraternity?" I ask. I want to clear this up right away. I know what people think of me, and I know the reputation that "frat guys" have around campus. But that's not me.

She tilts her head toward me, waiting for my answer.

"Because my best friend wanted in, and they would only take him if I joined. My dad was a legacy in the frat. I didn't want to, but I guess the more legacies that join, the more money they get for the house."

We approach the front of the library, and she stops, turning to face me.

"Is that true?" she asks. Her eyes are studying me, looking for the truth of my words.

"One hundred percent. I wouldn't lie to you, Ali. That's not me."

Her lips flatten as she considers me for a moment. I would love to know what is going through her mind but know that she is not ready for me to ask just yet.

I hold my hand out, motioning toward the door. I need her to trust me, and for some reason, I get the feeling that isn't something she readily gives.

After a few seconds, she nods and heads up the stairs.

Once inside, we head to one of the study rooms for some privacy. I know I don't want to discuss any type of romance scene where other people can hear. I write science fiction. Aliens, time travel, and parallel universes are my motif. I honestly don't know if I even know how to be romantic. My parents are still together, but I can't say that my dad has a single romantic bone in his body. Sure, he buys my mother flowers for their anniversary, but that's about it.

We both take out a notebook and pen.

"So, what do you know about romance?" I ask.

"Uh, not much," she says. "I guess we need a couple, right? That's what it's about – two people falling in love?"

I chuckle. "Yeah. Boy meets girl, boy and girl fall in love, and they live happily ever after. That's the extent of my knowledge of romance," I say, earning me the most adorable giggle ever.

"Okay. What kind of scene do you want to write? I know Marshall said we can make it as detailed as we want, but I honestly don't know if I have it in me to write about sex."

Her cheeks turn pink, and I watch as the color slowly creeps down her neck and into her shirt. I wonder how far down it goes.

Not the time, Cole. So not the time to have thoughts like that.

"Uh, yeah. I don't think I can either. I wouldn't know the first thing about sex anyway. It's not like I've ever had it."

The second the words leave her mouth she gasps and covers it with her hands, her eyes wide in shock.

"Oh, God. I need to go!" she says as she scrambles to her feet.

I jump up and grab her shoulders, trying to come up with something to say that will keep her here. "Wait! You have nothing to be embarrassed about, Ali. I'm right there with you."

She freezes at my confession but still refuses to meet my eyes.

"You don't have to say that to make me feel better, Cole. I know you probably have way more experience than me. Just look at you," she says.

I place my finger under her chin. Her skin is so soft, so delicate against the roughness of mine. She senses my intent and raises her face up, but her eyes flitter around the room looking everywhere but at me.

"Hey, look at me, Ali."

She shakes her head. "I'm going to email Professor Marshall and tell him to place us with other people. You shouldn't have to be stuck with me as your partner. I would ruin this grade for you."

"No way, Ali! I want to work with you. I think we will make a great team. And there's no better way to improve our writing than to challenge ourselves by stepping outside our comfort zones, right?" I ask. I am desperate to make this work with her. I don't know what it is about her, but I know that if I let her walk out that door, I won't get another chance to get to know her.

She is almost gasping for breath, and I hate the panic I see on her face. I wasn't kidding when I hinted that I was a virgin, too – at least that's what I think she was saying. People make a lot of assumptions, especially when you are in a fraternity. Yeah, I go to parties. I am a friendly person so if a girl approaches me, I'll talk to her. But I have never been serious enough about anyone to take it to the next level. My parents instilled the concept of being in love when you share that with a person, and I am holding strong to that concept.

I need to calm her down, so I do the only thing I can think of – I pull her into my arms.

Her entire body stiffens, but she doesn't resist. I pull her head to my chest and wrap the other around her waist. She feels so good against me and we fit perfectly. My chin rests on top of her head as she slowly melts into me.

My heart is racing but for a completely different reason than her frantic rhythm that is pounding against my palm. She is worried about being a virgin, while the only thing I am focused on is the fact that I think I finally found what I've been looking for.

Chapter 3
Ali

How do I always seem to get myself into these embarrassing situations?

Well, this one is because I essentially admitted to the hottest man I have ever seen that I am a virgin.

Perfect.

But I can't for the life of me figure out why I am wrapped in his arms. While it is possibly the most amazing feeling, to be cocooned in his embrace, it is also confusing. From my experience, people don't really go out of their way to comfort others. Yet here we are.

He eventually releases me, and I step back quickly, needing some distance.

"You okay?" he asks, his face a mask of concern.

Who is this guy?

I nod because I don't think my voice would work right now. That, and I don't trust what might pop out of my mouth. My stupid filter appears to be broken today.

He takes a cautious step toward me and forces my chin up with his finger. I bite my lip and will my brain to come up with something, anything to say that would make this all less humiliating.

"I'm sorry," I say. Not the worst thing I could say, but not the best either.

"You have nothing to be sorry about. Look, I get it. Neither of us wants to write romance. It's mortifying and not anywhere close to something in my wheelhouse. But, I think if we look at it as a way to become better writers, we can get through it. Together."

He's right. This is a good opportunity to challenge ourselves as writers, and I'm sure that between the two of us, we can come up with something at least remotely decent.

"Okay," I say, and he lets out a breath as if my approval is exactly what he wanted to hear.

We both take our seats again. I tap my pen anxiously against the dark wood of the table, chewing on my lips, a nervous habit I developed through the years. My knee is bouncing, and no matter how hard I try, I can't focus on anything other than the fact that I was just in his arms.

"I have a thought," he says after a few minutes of silence. "What if we both read a short romance book to give us an idea of what we need to accomplish?"

"That's actually not a bad idea."

"Don't sound so surprised," he teases and I wince.

"Sorry," I say for what feels like the hundredth time in the past hour.

He frowns. "You have to stop apologizing. You did nothing wrong."

I can't tell if I am aggravating him or annoying him. Or maybe it's something entirely different. I have no idea. I am completely out of my element here and the longer I am here, the more my anxiety builds.

He shakes his head at me. "Ok, well, back to my idea. The only problem is I have no clue how to figure out which book to read."

I laugh. "Oh, I have a way to find one. My friend, Laura, is a romance fanatic. I'm sure she can recommend one, or a thousand, that we could check out."

"Perfect. Why don't you reach out to her and then text me with the book? We can both read it over the next couple of days and then we can meet again to discuss it," he says.

"Sounds good." Does it though? Forcing myself to read a romance book is one thing, but getting together with Cole to discuss it is an entirely different problem. I already know I will be a mess - a bright red, blushing disaster, trying to talk about romance.

"Here. Give me your phone," he says, holding his hand out.

I do, and he adds himself as a contact.

"Do you want me to add my number to your contacts?" I ask. His eyes widen briefly, but he quickly recovers.

"Uh, you can just text me, and I'll have it," he says in a rush.

Weird. I wonder what that's about.

I shake my head and tell myself I'm just reading into things. I send him a quick text so that he has my number and we both gather our things. He holds his hand on the small of my back and we head outside. Once we are through the doors, he leads me to the side of the entryway. There are students bustling about as we come to a stop. Some wave or nod at Cole, but no one acknowledges me. It's like I'm not even here. I guess that's better than them wondering what he's doing with me.

We are both just staring at one another saying nothing. It's not a comfortable silence. The moment feels awkward and it's like I don't know how to say goodbye to someone.

"Uh, so, I'll text you once I hear back from Laura," I say, but it comes out so quickly that the words are jumbled together.

Cole nods and then pulls me into a hug. I hesitate for a moment, not sure what is happening. But I decide being back in his arms again is too good to pass up, so I throw my arms around his waist.

He seems reluctant to let me go, but I'm sure that is just wishful thinking on my part. There's no way someone as amazing as him would be into someone like me.

When he pulls back, he raises his hand and brushes a few loose strands of my hair behind my ear with his fingers. His touch lingers, but only briefly. "I'll see you soon, Ali."

"Uh, yeah. I'll see you."

With that, he turns and walks away.

I stand there and watch him, not sure what I am hoping to see, but I can't seem to tear my eyes away. This entire day has been so strange. Being paired with Cole was terrifying at first, but he somehow managed to make it comfortable. I am not normally one to take to new people easily, yet he made it seem so effortless. We just... clicked.

Right before he disappears around the corner of a building, Cole turns back around. I panic at being caught watching him, but he does something that surprises me. He smiles, widely, and waves.

Was he checking to see if I was still here?

A memory from high school floods my mind and I quickly turn and speed walk away without waving back. There is no way I am letting that happen again.

No freaking way.

Me: Hey. Any chance you can recommend a short, easy, romance book for me?

Laura: OMG!!!! Are you finally going to start writing romance? I've only been begging you for a year!

Me: Ha! No way. I have to write a romance scene for my class. My partner and I thought it might be good to read something since neither of us know anything about romance.

Laura: Your partner?

Me: Grrr. The professor paired us up for the final project.

Laura: Who is yours?

I pause. I know if I tell her who it is she will freak out. She knows I've had a crush on Cole for a while and she is constantly trying to get me to talk to him.

I sigh.

Me: Cole Buchanan.

My phone rings and I groan.

"Hello?"

"Are you fucking with me right now? You have been paired with Cole for a project and you two have to write a romance together?" Laura's very excited voice screeches into the phone so loudly that I have to pull it away from my ear.

"Yes."

"This is epic!" Her enthusiasm is so not what I need right now.

"No, it's torture. How am I supposed to write romance, of all things, with Cole?" I ask.

My guinea pigs, Han and Chewie, choose that moment to squeal in delight, as if they, too, are taking pleasure in my misery.

"Are you home?" Laura asks, obviously having heard the boys' outburst.

"Yes."

"I'm coming over. We have so much to talk about," she says and ends the call despite my protests.

I should have never said anything. The last thing I want to do is talk about this. I just want to do what I have to and get it over with as soon as possible. Then I can go back to my life and forget that this ever happened.

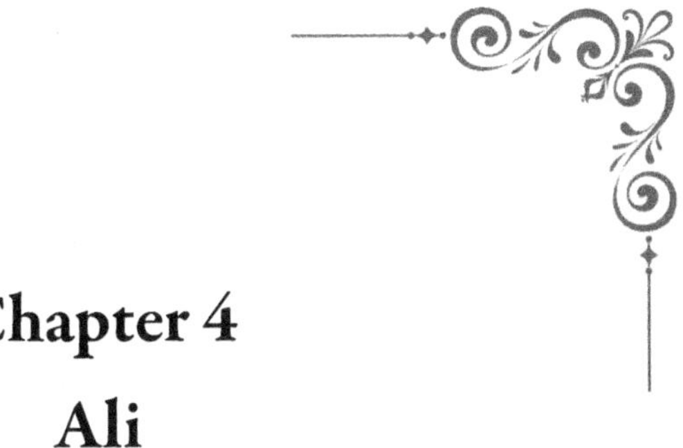

Chapter 4
Ali

"So, this one has a strong alpha male and some really great sex scenes," Laura says as she lays yet another romance book on my table. It is the tenth book she has pulled out, and the bag she brought is still overflowing.

"Alpha male? What the hell is that?" I ask.

She giggles. "Oh, Ali. I have so much to teach you."

We spend the next hour going over books and my mind feels ready to explode. Shifters, vampires, dominants... I am in way over my head here and don't know what to do.

She senses my discomfort and places a soft hand on my arm. "Ali. It will be fine." She reaches into her bag and hands me one final book. Unlike most of the other books that have half-naked men on the covers, this one has a couple with their arms wrapped around each other. Both are fully clothed, thankfully, and they are staring lovingly into each other's eyes with their foreheads pressed together.

"What's this?" I ask, taking the book.

"I saved the best for last. It's one of my favorites. A simple love story about an unlikely couple finding love. There are a few sex scenes, but they are sweet, and they will melt your heart. You will love it, I swear."

I eye her suspiciously, waiting for the punch line. "That's it. Two humans falling in love with a little bit of sex?"

"Yes, Ali. I know I like a wide range of things, but sometimes, a good *human* romance is all you need," she says, stressing the word human. It's probably because I scoffed at all the different tropes she pulled out of her bag. I mean, come on, one of the books actually had a dragon on the cover with a scantily clad female sitting on its back. It's not just me, right?

I flip the book back and forth. After I read the blurb on the back, I decide to give it a shot.

"Ok. But if I end up being thoroughly scandalized, I am blaming you!"

"Sure, sure. I will take full blame if you don't like it."

We say our goodbyes, and I am left alone with the book. I'm not sure if I should read it before I recommend it to Cole, or if I should just tell him and get it over with. It sounds simple enough, and it's less than a hundred pages so I'm sure we can both finish it quickly.

I throw caution to the wind and send him a text.

Me: After an hour of pure torture with Laura, I think I have a book for us to read.

Cole: Pure torture? Sound scandalous.

I laugh that he used the same word that I used with Laura.

Me: You don't even want to know...

Cole: I'm on the edge of my seat.

I send him a picture of the book and wait.

Cole: "When Eyes Meet". Just ordered it.

Me: Did you read the blurb?

Cole: Yeah. Doesn't sound too terrible.

Me: Well, it was either that or a book about a dragon shifter falling in love with the king's daughter. I made a gut decision.

Cole: Dragon shifter? Do tell.

I laugh again.

Me: Believe me, the less you know, the better.

Cole: Ok. This is pretty short. Why don't we meet on Thursday to discuss our expertise in romance after reading this book?

Me: Expertise? After one book? You must have really high expectations.

Cole: I guess we'll find out. I'll text you.

Me: Ok.

I put my phone down and reluctantly grab the book again.

Just read it, Ali. Don't be such a prude.

My pep talk does nothing for my nerves. I have no idea why the thought of reading this book about love gives me such anxiety. But if I'm being completely honest, it's not the book. It's the thought of having to discuss it with Cole that bothers me.

I can just picture it. Me sitting across from him, my face doing its best impersonation of a tomato. I will be a stuttering, blubbering mess. Not exactly how I want Cole to see me. The even bigger conundrum is why I even want Cole to see me at all. I do best blending into the background, going unnoticed. I learned the hard way that getting noticed isn't all it's cracked up to be. When people see you, they tend to do awful things to you.

Ali Eeew! What's wrong? Did you actually think this was serious? You're so gullible!

The voices haunt me every day. Being the center of attention is not something I ever wanted, but when it is at the expense of my dignity, it is the absolute worst.

I settle back on my couch, trying my best to get comfortable as I begin reading. I think back to when Cole said it "doesn't sound too terrible." I really hope he's right.

It's the way her eyes shine. The way she demands attention, even if it is the last thing she wants. I know she doesn't believe that I love her, but I'll be damned if I don't prove it to her.

"Let me kiss you. Please," I beg, aching to know how she tastes.

Her expressive eyes gaze at me warily, but she nods. It is all the permission I need as I press my lips to hers.

The initial touch is explosive, more than I ever imagined it would be. The first kiss to top all first kisses. Her lips are soft and inviting, but it is her gasp of pleasure that fuels the beast inside me.

I take advantage and dive in, pressing my tongue to hers, leading it in a sensual dance of desire.

This woman, this amazingly beautiful girl, is everything, and our kiss only proves that she is all I have ever wanted. Touching her is the most exhilarating experience. My heart is pounding, calling out to its one true love.

I have to force myself to pull back, but I need to make sure she is still with me, and not chasing the demons of her past in her mind.

"Are you okay, my beautiful butterfly?"

She smiles. "I had no idea it could feel like that."

I cup her cheek and rub my thumb across her bottom lip.

"This is just the beginning. It can be so much more if you will let me show you," I say softly.

What in the actual hell?

I absolutely despise myself for liking this book. I haven't finished it yet, but I have to put it down for a few minutes to recover. There is no way love is like that in real life. No man would ever speak to a woman so lovingly. Right?

I get the draw, the dream of finding someone to love you, to spend your life with. Someone you would count on for anything and everything. Someone who would do anything for you. But I have a hard time believing that anyone would go to such an extent to prove their love to someone. I mean, it is so unbelievable, so unrealistic.

The whole concept of an unlikely couple, of two people who have no business being together falling in love. It's almost laughable.

I hate to say it, but it would be like Cole falling for me.

If only...

Chapter 5
Cole

*"**I** need to be inside you, Michaela. I need to feel you wrapped around me," I say, knowing that if I don't have her soon, I won't survive.*

"Take me, Jaxson. Make me yours," she moans, and it is all the invitation I need.

My mouth finds hers and I groan at the taste. My hands roam down her body, cupping her full breasts. The sounds coming from her are only fueling the fire raging inside me as I fight for control. I have to force myself to slow down. This is about her, about showing her how much I love her, how much I need her.

I need to prove to her that she can trust me. I want to erase everything she has been through, all the hurt and betrayal, and replace it with happy memories. I want her to come to me if she needs anything, no matter what. I want to be her everything because she is mine.

I make quick work of removing her clothes. When she is completely bare before me, I rub my mouth and growl at the sheer beauty before me.

"I am going to devour you, butterfly," I say, running my fingers through her damp folds.

I can't wait any longer. I pull her to the end of the bed and lean down, placing my mouth right over her wet center. I become a beast as I take her to an entirely new level of pleasure. My entire focus is on making her feel good.

"Jaxson, I need more. I need...," she says in between gasps.

I pull back but don't go far. My lips brush against her sex as I speak. "What, butterfly? Tell me what you need and it's yours. I'll give you anything."

"I need you, Jaxson. I need you inside me. Make love to me," she says.

As much as I would love to live with my mouth between her legs, my need to be sheathed in her warmth is greater.

I crawl up her body slowly, nipping and kissing my way to her mouth.

"I absolutely adore you, butterfly," I say, kissing her. I know she can taste herself, and I love it.

I stare deep into her eyes as I line myself up, ready to finally make her mine.

With one thrust, I am overwhelmed with the most intense pleasure I have ever felt. I squeeze my eyes closed, fighting the urge to spill myself, it is just that good.

Holy shit!

I am slightly ashamed to admit that had I known romance books were this intense, I might have tried reading one a long time ago.

I am aroused... harder than I have ever been. I know the author described how the characters looked in the beginning, but the only thing I can picture as I read is Ali. Her golden-brown hair, her chocolate eyes, her curves... damn, I either need to take a cold shower or read some more.

Fuck. How am I going to talk about this book with her when I can't even read it without getting all flustered? There is no way I will be able to sit across from her, staring at her luscious body, and have a serious conversation. One thing is certain, we will need to be sitting down, preferably at a table, that will cover the erection I know I will have the entire time.

It has been two days since I last saw her, but she has filled my thoughts every second since. Those two days have felt like an eternity. I have to restrain myself from texting her every minute and it is pure torture. I want to know what she is doing, who she is with, and how her day is going. I need to know that she is safe, that she is happy.

I don't know where these feelings are coming from, but I honestly don't care because they feel right. From the first moment I looked into her eyes, everything became clear.

Fuck, I am starting to sound like the dude from the romance novel.

I close the book and toss it away from me. It lands on the floor with a thud just as the door to my room flies open and bangs against the wall.

"What are you doing hiding in your room? We could use your help planning the mixer this weekend," Trevor says. He's my best friend, the one that wanted to join this stupid fraternity. The only reason I am here.

The two of us became friends back in middle school when his family moved to town. We have been through a lot together. He spent a good portion of his time at my house, especially after his parents got divorced. His father was a mean son of a bitch, and once his mom took off, he turned his attention to Trevor. My parents took him in without question and helped him press charges against his dad. What started out as just making sure he had a place to stay while it all went down turned into him living with us full-time.

He's my brother for all intents and purposes. I would do anything for him, hence, why I am living in this stupid frat house.

"Just getting some schoolwork done," I say.

His eyes land on the romance book that is laying face up in the middle of my floor and he smirks.

"When Eyes Meet, huh? Branching off into romance, brother?" he asks in a teasing voice.

"Fuck off. It's for a class," I say.

There is a moment of stillness and we both glance back and forth between each other and the book. I don't know how, but we dive for it at the same time, and it turns into a massive wrestling match for possession of the offending object.

His elbow catches me in the gut, and he quickly gains control, jumping to his feet with it in his hands. I am still gasping for breath on my back as he begins to read whatever page he opened it to.

"Dude. This is like book porn," he says, his eyes widening at whichever passage he is reading. "Were you jerking off to this shit?"

"Fuck you, no. I was not jerking off. I told you; I have to read it for a class."

"What class has you reading this smut?"

I roll my eyes. "What do you think, dumbass? Writing."

"So... you're telling me that in order to become a better sci-fi writer, you have to read a sex book?"

I growl. There is no way he will understand. He's into computers and programming. He won't get the concept of broadening your horizons. I just shrug.

"Hey, man. No judgement here. Just surprised is all. Whatever you have to do."

He hands me the book and turns to leave. Just when I think I am free, he turns back.

"Does this have anything to do with that Ali chick you've been pining over?"

I narrow my eyes at him. "What are you talking about?" I have never spoken to him about Ali before, and I wouldn't. I'm not that guy that feeds off discussing my love life. I know a lot of the guys here love to share details of their latest conquests. Very graphic details. It is beyond disrespectful to any of the girls, but they don't care. It's one of the most frustrating things about living here. I hate knowing what they do to those poor girls. Don't get me wrong, it's all consensual, but it's all about scoring to these guys.

"Okay, okay. Play innocent all you want, but I know you, man. I see the way you watch her whenever we see her around campus. Mister virgin. Mister saving himself for 'the one'. It's great and all, but you need to either shit or get off the pot man. She's hot," he says, and I growl. He holds his hands up in front of him. "I'm just saying. If you don't make a move, someone else will. And I don't want to see you get hurt."

I glare at him, hating that he's right, about everything. Ali is more than hot. She's beautiful, gorgeous even. Everything about her calls to me, and probably every other male on this campus and everywhere else. But it's her eyes that really get me. Chocolate with hints of caramel so brown that I could get lost just staring into them. They are so expressive, so innocent. They show exactly who she is, the overwhelming goodness in her heart. And don't even get me started on how they look when she smiles. They shine, brighter than any star, fully displaying her warmth.

"I know how beautiful she is. I just didn't know you did," I say in a grumble.

"Cole, you need to take a chance and tell her how you feel. Ask her out or something. You never know how she'll react if you don't try."

"When did you become a romantic?"

He chuckles. "Believe me. I'm not. Far from it. I wouldn't know the first thing about wooing a girl. You do remember where I come from, right?" he asks solemnly.

"Sorry, man. I didn't mean anything by it," I say quickly.

He holds his hand up to stop me. "I know. I'm just saying you deserve to be happy. You've been there for me through everything. It's my turn to have your back."

With that, he turns and leaves.

I'm lost in thought for a while, staring at the wall as if it will give me the answers. It would kill me to see Ali with someone else, but in the same sense, unless I do something, I have no claim over her.

With that in mind, I grab my phone.

It's time for me to take a chance.

Me: How are you liking the book?

Chapter 6
Ali

And, as I stare into her ocean-blue eyes, I realize that she is everything I have ever wanted. I never knew you could feel so much for one person. My heart feels like it is going to explode with love.

"I love you, Michaela. I love you with every single part of me, and I want to spend the rest of my life taking care of you. I want you to be mine, only mine, and I want to be yours. You hold my heart in your hands. You have control of my entire future."

The fear that I see staring back at me almost breaks me. I can sense her hesitation and can feel her nervousness at my confession. I have told her I love her. She has heard it many times over the past few weeks. But I have never laid it all on the line like I am doing right now. Everything from her past is doing its best at preventing any possible future that we have together.

"I'm scared, Jaxson," she says in a whisper.

Her words cut right to my heart. "I could never, would never hurt you, Michaela. It's not possible. You own me, every piece of me."

She closes her eyes, taking slow, measured breaths as she contemplates my promise.

I cup her cheeks, forcing her to look at me as I do the only thing I can to convince her I am telling her the truth.

The second her eyes meet mine, I smile. "Marry me."

"What?"

"Marry me. Let me prove to you how much I mean everything I am saying, how much I love you. Let me spend the rest of my life worshipping you."

"You're crazy!"

"Crazy is a great place to live. I'll show you," I say, taking her in the most love-filled, emotional kiss of my life.

My phone buzzing catches me off guard and I jump. I am almost mad at being ripped away from one of the most romantic things I have ever read. Don't tell Laura – I would deny it until my last breath.

I grab my phone angrily but stop short when I see it is a text from Cole.

Cole: How are you liking the book?

Uh... I'm not really sure I should answer that honestly. I despise the fact that this book is making me long for a little romance myself.

I decide to keep my answer vague.

Me: It's not what I was expecting.

I watch as the little text bubble pops up, then disappears, then pops up again repeatedly for a long time. Either he has a lot to say about it or he can't decide how to say it. I'm not sure which would be better.

Cole: You can say that again. I don't think I can write anything close to this.

I blush at the thought of Cole bent over his laptop trying to write something with as much heat in this book.

Me: We are in way over our heads, aren't we?

I almost drop my phone when it rings, Cole's name on the screen.

How can I both want to answer it, and want to flush my phone down the toilet at the same time?

"Hello?" I answer, hating how shaky my voice sounds.

"Hey, Ali." The smooth cadence of his voice is both soothing and exhilarating. My pulse is hammering, making it hard to breathe.

"We can't do this, can we?" I ask, voicing my true concern.

My entire life, the only thing I have ever wanted was to write. My very first memories are of stories I used to make up and tell my dad. He would sit and listen to me for hours, talking about whatever I was obsessed with at the time. It ranged from dragons to princesses, to aliens and beyond. I had the most active imagination and my father used to call me his little novelist.

"Ali, we'll be fine. I won't let you fail. I promise," he says, and for some reason, I believe him.

"Did you finish it?" I ask.

He chuckles. "Not yet. I had to put it down for a bit."

"Why?" I ask, not sure I understand.

"Uh... it was a bit... uh... more than I expected." He sounds nervous and flustered.

"Mor... oh." He was aroused.

Shit. So was I, but I can't admit that to him of all people.

"Yeah. Oh. I have never read anything like that before. Some of the books I have read have had relationships in them, but *nothing* like that."

I clear my throat, my mouth suddenly very dry. "Yeah. I know what you mean."

"Did you get flustered reading it, Ali?"

"Wha... what?"

His voice drops, sounding deeper than ever. "Did you like reading the sex scenes?"

"I, uh, I'm not sure, um..." I stammer, sounding like a complete idiot.

"It's okay if you did. It's a normal reaction, like watching porn."

"I have never watched porn," I say, completely shocked at my words. What the hell is wrong with me? I can't filter the words from my brain when Cole is involved.

"Well, you should. But I'll be honest, it has nothing on the scenes from this book. I don't think I have ever been that hard before. Those parts were pretty fucking amazing," he says.

Oh. My. Freaking. Snot! Is he seriously talking about this with me right now?

"Did I say too much?" he asks, and I still can't find words. Even if I could, I'm not sure that my voice would work right now with how little air I am pulling into my lungs.

"Ali?" he asks, but his voice is softer this time.

"No," I manage to say.

"No, what, Ali?"

Why does he have to keep saying my name? And why, for the love of all things, does it have to sound so sensual coming from his mouth?

"No, you didn't say too much. And yes."

He groans. It's barely audible like he pulled the phone away from his ear. He knows what I am saying, but I know he is going to push me to verbalize it.

"Yes, what, Ali? Say it."

Why did I have to say it? Why couldn't I just keep my mouth shut?

I take a deep breath. "Yes," I say, barely a whisper. "Yes, I liked those parts. Yes, I was aroused."

This time, his moan is loud, like he can't contain it.

"Tell me, Ali. How did it make you feel?"

I pull the phone away from my ear and stare at it like it is my phone's fault I am in this situation. Granted, there are far worse things that could be happening. Well, at least I assume there are. I am having a really hard time accepting the fact that I am having a conversation with Cole freaking Buchanan about sex.

And yet, here I am.

"Uh," I say. Nice, Ali. Real classy. The man asks you how you felt and all you can say is "uh". Smooth. I'm sure he is really turned on now, not that I want him to be turned on. Or, do I? Yup, I'm drowning here.

"Did it make you wet, Ali?"

Seriously, if he could just stop saying my name I would be able to think!

I let out a little squeak. Yup, I am seriously the least sexy person alive.

I remain silent, unable to form a coherent thought. Cole isn't saying anything either, and I don't know if it's because I ruined this entire thing, or something else.

After a few minutes, I check my phone to make sure he didn't hang up on me. The call is still active, but it is silent... until it isn't.

There is heavy breathing that comes through, and it makes everything more intense.

"Cole?" I ask, but I'm not sure what I am asking exactly.

"Yeah, angel eyes?"

Angel eyes? What is happening?

I curl my legs up underneath my body. I am leaning deep into the corner of my couch more than overwhelmed by this conversation. Between the sex talk, the noises he is making, and now the nickname, I am more than... flustered, as he called it.

"Are you okay?" I ask.

"No. I can't stop thinking about this book and how it is making me feel. Maybe that makes me a pussy to admit, but it has opened my eyes, that's for damned sure."

"It doesn't make you a pussy," I say. "A lot of guys read romances."

"I'm not talking about the book, Ali. I'm talking about admitting my feelings."

"I don't understand."

He lets out a laugh, but it is filled with frustration, not humor. "I mean how I feel about you."

I gulp. He can't be serious. I hate that my first thought is that he is messing with me, but experience takes precedence over the present. It always will. I will never forget what I went through, and I refuse to let it happen again.

"You're messing with me," I say, my voice coming out a hell of a lot stronger than I feel.

"I'm not. I like you, Ali."

Nope. Not going there again.

"I think we should focus on the project, Cole."

"Why?"

"Because it's what's best," I say, not really meaning it. I would love to entertain the idea that Cole could possibly consider me that way, but why bother? I would only end up with a broken heart, and more embarrassment.

Been there, done that, pretty sure I have a gold medal in it.

"I disagree," he says more forcefully.

"Look, I'll reserve us a study room at the library tomorrow so we can write our scene."

"Ali," he starts, but I interrupt him.

"I'll text you the time. Goodbye, Cole," I say and end the call.

I know I made a sensible decision. I do.

But why does it feel like I just tore my own heart out and stomped on it?

Chapter 7
Cole

She's scared.

She's afraid to admit that she feels something for me.

Someone hurt her, that much I can tell, but what I can't figure out is how to get her to give me a chance.

While I wait for her text, I finish the book. It ends, of course, with the grand gesture from Jaxson, and he and Michaela ride off into the figurative sunset together.

Huh. A grand gesture.

Maybe that's what I need to do for Ali. No, she's not ready for that. I need her to trust me first.

Right as I am about to head to the shower, she sends me a text to meet her at the library at six o'clock tomorrow.

Me: I'm sorry.

I keep it short, rather than pouring my heart out in a text. I didn't mean to push her earlier, but I felt like she was there with me. She was breathing heavily, her voice was soft and timid. She was turned on, but I think I pushed too far. I got caught up in the moment, in the heat of the book. I stepped over the line.

She doesn't respond right away, and I worry that I blew any shot I ever had with her. My finger is hovering over the call button, knowing full well that she wouldn't answer, but I have to try. Just as I am about to push it, her text comes through.

Ali: You don't need to apologize.

Me: I do. I took it too far.

I'm typing out a more detailed response, but she cuts me off.

Ali: I'll see you tomorrow.

My heart aches with her answer. I want to hope she is keeping this short because she is embarrassed about what happened. She has no reason to feel that way, but I get it. We are both virgins, I think. Neither of us knows what we are doing. Sure, as I told her, I have watched porn, but that doesn't mean I would be able to perform well if given the chance.

Man, I really want the chance. But only with her.

I would like to think I could figure out how to please her, how to make her feel good. Shit, for all I know I would not be able to make her come at all.

I grab my stuff and head to the shower, needing a nice cold one. As I stand under the stream of water, I can't help but remember the breathiness of her voice. I could feel her arousal through the phone, and I would have given anything to see the flush of her skin, because I know it was there. I can just imagine the way her pupils would be dilated, the brightness of her eyes as she experienced the high of her orgasm.

Fuck. Just the thought of it has me harder than a baseball bat. I take myself in hand as I turn the water hot. I brace myself with one arm on the wall of the shower as I stroke myself to the thoughts of Ali. In my mind, she is on her knees in front of me, ready to take me in her mouth. Her angel eyes stare up at me, the innocence pouring off her.

"Take me in your hands, Ali," I moan softly to my vision.

My hand pumps faster as I picture her leaning forward and running her tongue up my length. I sigh loudly as I grip myself harder.

"That's it. Just like that. Show me those angel eyes. Let me see you look at me as you stroke me," I mumble.

Fuuuuuuck. Dream Ali has me so close. I can almost hear her whimpers of pleasure as she moves her head up and down. Just as I am about to explode, I picture her hand finding her own core, rubbing furiously as she sucks the very life out of my cock.

I detonate and spray my seed all over the wall of the shower, biting my fist to prevent myself from calling out her name. My body sags, completely spent from the amazing dream, yet it is terribly disappointed that it wasn't real.

It may never be real if I don't fix the damage I have done.

I have to make this right.

I need to make her see I can be what she needs, that we can be great together.

How? I have no idea. But I'll be damned if I let her slip through my fingers again.

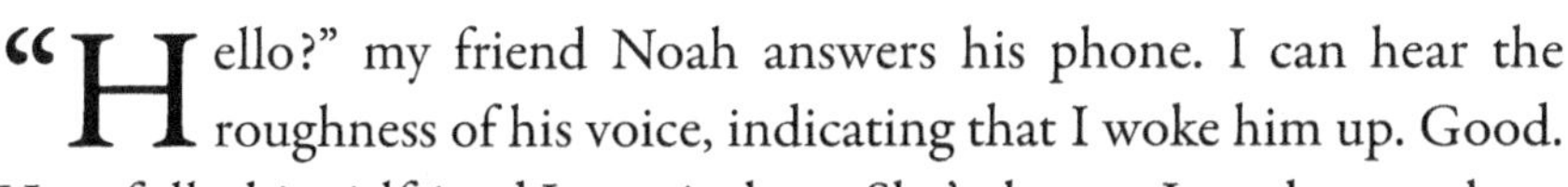

"Hello?" my friend Noah answers his phone. I can hear the roughness of his voice, indicating that I woke him up. Good. Hopefully, his girlfriend Laura is there. She's the one I need to speak to.

"Hey, Noah. Is Laura with you?" I ask.

"Cole? Fuck, man. You know what time it is?" He's pissed, but I don't care right now.

"Yeah, I know it's early. But I really need Laura."

"What the fuck? Why do you need to speak to my woman?" Now he's really pissed.

"Listen. I don't have time to get into it with you. It's about one of her friends," I say, getting frustrated at this back-and-forth.

I hear him speaking to Laura. "Here, babe. It's Cole. I think he's on drugs or something. He wants to talk to you."

I would laugh at his assumption if I wasn't so desperate.

"Cole? What's wrong?" Laura asks, sounding just as sleepy as Noah.

"Hey, Laura. Sorry to wake you," I say, and hear Noah in the background. "Hmph. Didn't apologize to me."

"It's okay. What's going on?"

"I need to talk to you about Ali."

Her voice takes on a new tone, one of pure concern. "Oh, my god. What happened to Ali? Is she okay?"

"Yes, she's fine. I just fucked up, and I need to know how to fix it."

"What do you mean you fucked up? What did you do to her? Did you hurt her? Shit, Cole, I'll rip your dick off if you hurt her," she threatens, and I hear Noah growl.

"Don't even joke about touching another man's dick, babe."

I am about ready to scream. These two need to focus.

"Laura, please," I say, and even I can hear the desperation in my voice.

"Tell me everything, Cole. And don't leave anything out. You want my help with Ali, I need the truth," she says. Her tone is serious yet somehow holds a note of hostility. I remember her earlier threat about a spoon and my balls and I involuntarily shiver.

So, I tell her everything from how I have wanted Ali for longer than I care to admit, to our project, to the book, to the texting and phone conversations. Everything.

"Wow," she says.

"Wow? That's all you can give me after I just completely poured my heart out."

"Sorry, Cole. I just had no idea. I mean, I knew she had a crush on you, but..."

"What? She likes me?" I say, completely cutting her off.

"Uh, what? No. I didn't say that," she says nervously.

"Yeah, you did." I couldn't stop the smile that takes over my face, even if I tried.

"Shit." She sighs, loudly. "You can't tell her I told you. She would kill me. I mean, literally, murder me."

"I won't. Tell me how to fix this, Laura. I can't lose her." *Not that I had her to begin with.* But I don't say that part.

"Be honest with her. Tell her how you feel," she says.

"I kind of already did that."

"Kind of? Come on, Cole. You have to be completely honest. Lay it all on the line. With what she's been through, she needs to know she can trust you."

"Wait. What has she been through? What happened to her?" I ask frantically. I'll kill anyone that hurt her.

"Shit. Forget I said that," she says.

"Can't do that, Laura. Tell me what happened. Tell me what motherfucker I have to find and hurt."

"No way. That's her story to tell. It's one thing to let it slip that she wants you, it's a completely different story to betray her trust. That I won't do, no matter what you say," she says.

"What do I do, Laur? Tell me what to do to make her trust me," I plead.

"You can't make her trust you. Trust is earned, not given," she says. I think about that for a minute. It reminds me of something my mom once said to me. Something about how trust takes a long time to build, but only seconds to break, and a long time to fix. But I don't have a long time. Something tells me Ali won't give me much time to prove myself to her.

"I need her, Laura," I say quietly, the words filled with the angst and longing I feel.

Silence fills the line, but it is louder than anything I have ever heard. Without saying it, Laura is telling me how tough the road is that is set before me. It won't be easy.

"Show her, Cole. Prove it to her. She wants to believe it. I know she does. But she needs you to help her understand that you will be there no matter what. That's what matters to her."

I end the call, not able to speak.

What the fuck happened to Ali to hurt her so badly? Whatever it is, whatever walls she has built around her heart are about to be shattered. I won't give up on her. I can feel the connection between us. It is an invisible pull, drawing me to her.

Well, Ali, you'd better hang on because I am coming. I am one persistent bastard when it comes to the things I want, and I won't give up.

Chapter 8
Ali

I have to cancel. I can't do this. There is no way I can face him after everything that happened last night.

I want to believe what he was saying. That he is attracted to me. That he likes me. But I've been there before. I believed a lie and paid the price. And believe me... it was a heavy price. In fact, it was one of the worst experiences of my life. I haven't trusted anyone since.

Except for Laura, but it took an entire year of living together to get there. I kept waiting for the other shoe to drop. I couldn't believe that she was really my friend. But she stuck with me, even with all my doubts, she was there.

But it is totally different with Cole because of how much I already care for him. I'm not sure how it happened, especially since the other day was the first time I actually spoke to him in person. The thing is you can learn a lot about someone just by watching them. And I watched him, a lot.

He was always smiling. Kind and friendly with everyone. He seems so genuine, so real. But, as I learned, even that can be deceiving.

My focus is on the clock on my wall as the minutes tick by, putting me closer and closer to our meeting.

The only reason I haven't canceled is that my grade depends on this. Silly, I know, but I need a good recommendation from Professor Marshall if I want to pursue my master's degree.

I can do this. I can be professional for an hour so that we can complete this scene. I have already decided to put my foot down and insist that this be a bland, vanilla romance scene. We can make it about the beginning of the relationship. There is no need to go into the details of what happens after the fact. That is usually where things get messy, where life gets in the way.

Where feelings get hurt.

I gather my things when it's time and make the slow trek across campus to the library. I reserved a room because this definitely needs to happen privately. I expect Cole to push about what happened last night, but I refuse to go there with him. What's done is done. We were both aroused. We were both caught up in everything. That's all it was. He said things out of desperation, to get me to continue the game. But I don't want to play anymore.

The sight of him sitting in the room waiting for me sets me on edge. When our eyes meet, I flinch at the sorrow I see in his.

No. Don't go there. Go in, sit down, and write. It's what you do best.

He doesn't say anything as I sit across from him and pull out my notepad. He has his laptop out and ready to go, but I am more of an old-fashioned girl, preferring pen and paper when I write.

I clear my throat and try to sound confident. "So, I was thinking that we could write our scene about the moment the couple meets for the first time. We can include the inner monologue of the female or male, depending on which point of view you want to go with..." I say in one breath, completely rambling, but stop short when I feel his hand take mine.

"Ali, can we talk about this?" he asks softly. I can feel the tension through his touch. It's like he would shatter with the slightest tap.

I pull my hand back. "There's nothing to talk about, Cole. Let's just get this scene written and be done. With everything."

He scoots his chair closer to me. The metal feet let out a horrific screech against the old linoleum floor.

I still haven't made eye contact since sitting down. I can't. It would only make this worse.

"Ali, please. Talk to me," he says, and it comes out as a hopeless plea.

I turn my head and stare at the bookshelf against the wall. Why? Why does he have to prolong this torture? Nothing is ever going to happen between us. It doesn't make sense. *We* don't make sense.

"What do you want me to say, Cole? Why are you doing this?" I ask. The hurt that I am feeling inside pours out through my words.

"Who hurt you, angel eyes? Who did this to you?"

At that, my head whips around and I glare at him. "No one. No one hurt me."

He slides even closer and now his knees are pressed against the outsides of my legs, effectively blocking any escape.

"I don't know what happened to you, but it's in the past. I would never hurt you, Ali. I can't."

"Sometimes the greatest lessons we can learn come from the past," I say dryly.

It's true. Experience tells us a lot.

"You can't let your past determine your future. The best thing you can do is learn from it and move on," he says, and I hate that it makes sense.

"You don't know anything," I say with a growl.

"Then tell me. Tell me what happened so I can help you."

I push back from him, freeing my legs. "Why are you pushing this? I obviously don't want to talk about it, and you are making things worse!"

"We need to trust each other so that we can work together."

Why do I get the feeling he is talking about more than our project?

I stand and turn away from him, not able to handle the intensity of his stare. Ironic, isn't it? The book we read was all about what can happen when you really take the time to look into someone's eyes. There is so much that you can see there.

But I can't deal with the emotions that his eyes hold.

"It was a long time ago, Cole. It doesn't matter." My voice sounds weak and defeated, and I loathe it.

The heat of his body seeps into my back as he comes to stand right behind me.

"If it is still affecting you this much, it does matter."

My chin drops to my heaving chest, and I am seriously fighting the urge to just run away.

Can I do this? Can I tell him and trust that he won't hurt me? I don't think there is a right answer here. I know what I feel, but that is completely different from what I want or need. I want to trust him. I want to believe that he won't hurt me. But I am terrified to open myself up to anyone.

My shoulders slump in defeat as I come to the realization that he will not let this go. Maybe I can just tell him, and we can move on. Maybe if he hears what they did to me, he'll understand that I'm a lost cause and we can just finish the project and go on with our lives.

"I was a nerd in high school. Well, I'm still a nerd, but that's beside the point. In my junior year, I started to get a lot of attention - attention I didn't want. There were a few of the seniors from the basketball team that started talking to me, all at the same time. They would each approach me at different times throughout my day. It seemed innocent enough. They would ask me how I was, about classes, and what I was doing that weekend. After a week or so, I started to gain some confidence. I would chat with each of them, just being friendly.

There was one guy on the team that hadn't spoken to me. Matt. He was the classic all-American boy. Blonde hair. Blue eyes. Tall. Muscular. He had been dating one of the popular girls in school for years, but I had heard that they had broken up. I wasn't boy-crazy, that was never my thing. But I would have been stupid to not notice how attractive he was."

Cole lets out a little growl, but I ignore him and continue.

"Well, one day, a couple of weeks after this all started, my friend, Amy, came running up to me excitedly. She told me that Matt had approached her and asked for my phone number. He told her he wanted to call me and get to know me. I remember feeling excited. I mean, here I was, the little, timid, nerd, getting attention from one of the most popular guys in school. And a senior at that."

I can hear the bitterness in my tone. Reliving this nightmare is not something I want to do. The only other person here at school who knows what happened is Laura, and that's only because I knew I could trust her.

"Go on, Ali. Finish it," Cole encourages.

I squeeze my eyes closed. I can still feel the embarrassment. "He called me a few nights later. The conversation wasn't that long, but it was sweet. Or at least I thought it was. I am still not sure how, but he got me to say some pretty personal things. I told him I never thought someone like him could be into someone like me. He asked what I meant, and I answered... stupidly. I told him I thought I was a nobody, that I was ugly and awkward and weird. I admitted how handsome I thought he was, and how I wanted to get to know him better. He asked me if anyone had ever kissed me before, and I was honest. I had been kissed once, but it was terrible. He asked me to describe what happened, and I did, telling him how I thought I was terrible at it, that I didn't know what I was doing."

I'm sure at this point, Cole can sense where this is going, but he's wrong. Nothing he could imagine could be worse than what happened.

And he's about to hear it all.

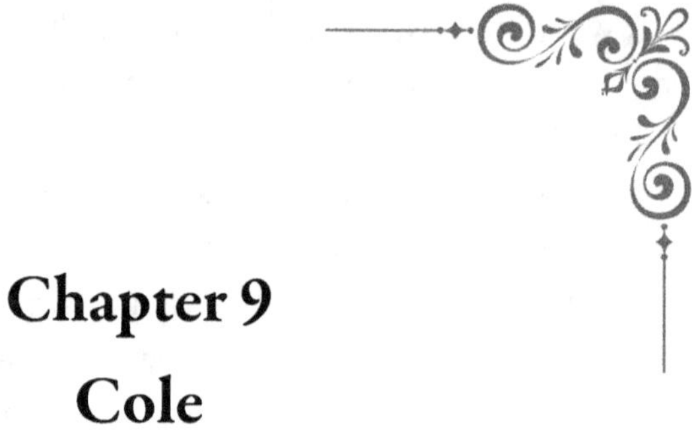

Chapter 9
Cole

The more she tells me, the hotter my blood boils. I can only guess where this is going, and all I want to do is find this Matt asshole and tear his throat out for doing this to her.

I want nothing more than to pull her into my arms and hold her, but that's not what she needs right now. It goes against everything in me, but I stand back and allow her to finish her story.

"He ended the call by telling me he would sit with me at lunch the next day at school. But that didn't happen." She pauses and takes a deep breath, and my stomach churns. If it is this hard for her to say, there is more damage done than I thought. "The next morning, I was sitting in homeroom when the morning announcements came on. But instead of the normal announcements, it was a recording, of my entire conversation with Matt. Every horrid detail, every single confession, every word I said was played over the loudspeaker, and the entire school heard it."

She sniffles and I can't take it any longer. I turn her to face me and pull her into my arms. She fights me at first, but after a few moments of me stroking her hair and whispering sweet words of apology into her ear, she relaxes into me. I thought her story was done, but I was wrong. She says the last part into my chest. "Everyone was laughing at me. Every class, every step I took in the hallway was torturous. They started calling me Ali Eeeew. *Everyone* called me that for the rest of high school."

"I'm so sorry that happened to you, Ali. So damn sorry," I say, because what else is there. People can be so mean, so wretched. She didn't deserve that. No one deserves to be treated like that.

We stand there for a while, just holding each other. I let her cry into my chest, and I do my best to console her. I hate what she went through. High school is hard enough, but it is even worse when you don't fit in. The fact that this was orchestrated, that it was obviously planned out makes it so much worse. Those guys went into this with the intention of hurting her, and she was targeted because she was not popular.

I ache for this poor woman. She is so strong to have made it through that alone, and I tell her as much.

"I'm not strong, Cole. Far from it," she says in a whisper.

I pull back, but only far enough to cup her cheeks. My thumbs caress her soft skin, wiping away the tears, the physical evidence of her pain. "Ali, you are amazing. What those guys, those assholes did to you, was deplorable. If I could, I would kick all their asses for messing with you. But you are still here, standing strong."

She pushes back from me, anger painting her beautiful face. "I'm standing strong, Cole? I can barely make it through each day! I am terrified that everyone I meet has an ulterior motive, that even though I don't know them, they are plotting something against me. Even you! Every single cell in my body is telling me to run away from you as fast as I can and don't look back, because if you ever did something like that to me, it would destroy me. I wouldn't survive."

"Ali... angel eyes, look at me," I say stepping into her. Her chin is tucked into her chest again as she swipes angrily at her tears. I reach out tentatively, not wanting to scare her. I cup her chin and raise it. My heart breaks once I see her eyes.

They are prominently displaying so many emotions. Fear, anger, worry... but there is one other thing there. Hope. There is a part of her that wants to believe that I would never hurt her, and that is the part that I try to reach.

"I swear on my life, I would never hurt you. It would be like tearing out my own heart, Ali." I take her hand and press it to my chest. "Feel that. Feel how hard it is pounding. I know you don't know me very well; I know you don't trust me yet, but I am asking you to give me a chance to prove it to you. Let me show you who I am."

Her lips tremble as she closes her eyes. But she doesn't lower her hand.

If ever there were a time that I wish one of my plotlines were true, it is now. The last story I wrote had a character who could read minds. If only she could read mine. She would know how serious I am right now.

Her resolve is wavering, and I don't want to lose the little progress I think we have made today.

"Let's get out of here," I say. "Let's go get something to eat and just relax."

"What about the project?" she asks.

"Fuck the project. We have plenty of time to get it done."

"I don't want to be around people right now," she says. I know she is feeling extremely vulnerable right now after telling me her story, and I don't blame her one bit. I would invite her back to my place, but I know the guys are having a party right now.

"I would say we could go to my place, but the guys are partying tonight."

She nods. "You could..." she starts but stops quickly as if she scared herself.

I step closer. "I could what?" I can only hope that she was about to invite me back to her place, where we can be alone.

Her breathing picks up to the point where she looks like she is about to hyperventilate, but after one final deep breath, she answers. "You could come back to my apartment."

I smile. "I would love that. We could pick up a pizza, or some Chinese food. Whatever you want. I just want to talk."

She nods and turns to pack up her things. I all but toss my laptop in my bag and stand, waiting for her. She is taking her time, but I can be patient. I know she is likely giving herself a pep talk, building up the nerve to do this.

When she stands, I hold out my hand to her. She stares at it for a minute before she takes it, and I want to pump my fist in the air.

I lead her outside and take the first steps forward in our relationship.

"You can't be serious!" she says between laughs.

We are back at her place, sitting on her couch with several containers of Chinese food sitting open on the table in front of us. I let her pick the food, and we decided to order a bunch of stuff and split it. We have been pigging out and laughing the entire time, some random TV show on quietly in the background.

I just told her how one time, back in high school, I ended up accidentally setting the school on fire.

"I wish I were kidding. Needless to say, I ended up switching out of the class right after that. We were a few months into the school year, but after that, they had no problem rearranging my schedule."

She is gasping for breath with how hard she is laughing. "How did you cause a fire making tuna melts of all things?"

I chuckle. "Let's just say I decided I would be able to toast the bread faster if I added oil to the pan. When I put the tray in the oven and set the temperature at 500 degrees, to make it cook faster, of course, it didn't take long for the oil to burst into flames."

Her hand is covering her mouth as she giggles, and it is the sweetest sound I have ever heard. "You are so beautiful," I say. I didn't mean for the words to come out, but I couldn't help it. Her smile could brighten anyone's day.

Her laughter dies off as she stares at me. "Don't."

"Don't what?"

"Don't say things you can't possibly mean."

The mood has completely shifted. Gone is the light, fun air that was surrounding us. It has been replaced by what can only be described as sexual tension mixed with disbelief.

"Why can't I mean it? You have no idea what I am thinking," I say as I reach out and tuck some loose hair behind her ear.

She turns away and busies herself with cleaning up, but I don't let her. I grab her hands and turn her back to face me, scooting as close as I can so that our legs are pressed together.

"I can't," she says.

"Can't what? Tell me why you are scared."

I stare deep into her eyes, willing her to open herself up to me, to allow me in her heart.

"It's too much," she whispers.

"That's what makes it good, angel eyes. Taking the leap is the best part of any adventure. You just have to take the first step."

I reach up and cup her cheek. When she leans into my touch, I realize it's now or never.

I have no idea if it is the right time or the worst decision I could possibly make, but I can't wait another second. I lean forward and press my lips to hers. She doesn't immediately pull away, or slap me into next Tuesday, so I take that as the green light.

My tongue comes out and licks her bottom lip, sliding across it slowly. A shudder works its way through her body as she raises her hands to my chest and fists my shirt.

I no longer have control of my body. I know this, because, without any thought whatsoever, I grip her hips and haul her into my lap so that she is straddling me. She tenses for a moment but then leans into me, her tongue finding its way into my mouth.

I groan at the first taste of her. It is a mixture of the saltiness of the food we just ate and the sweetness that is simply her. I have an overwhelming need to flip her under me, but I fight it, knowing full well she is not ready for that. Her hands find their way into my hair, and she fists it, pulling hard and sending a jolt throughout my body. The slight pain only fuels my desire for her.

She begins to rock against me, and that is my cue to slow things down. As much as I want to feel her sliding back and forth against my hardness, I don't want to go too far too fast.

My hands grip her hips and halt her movements as I slow the kiss. When I pull back, it is only to rest my forehead against hers.

We are both panting as we try to come down from the high of being together. I can almost feel her mind working, so I do what I do best and try to lighten the mood.

"Well, I don't think we will have any problem describing kissing in our scene. That was fucking amazing!"

She giggles and I feel the tension leave her body as she leans into me, resting her head on my shoulder. I wrap my arms around her and hold her close. She is tucked firmly against my chest, her hands resting between us as I run my fingers up and down her back.

"Thank you." She says it so quietly, I don't know if she realizes she even spoke out loud.

I can't imagine a more perfect moment than this.

Chapter 10
Ali

Cole: When can I see you again?

I giggle. He acts like we haven't spent every single evening together for the past week.

We worked on our scene, watched movies, and just cuddled. Yes, cuddled. Who knew that the big, muscular Cole would be a giant teddy bear on the inside?

Ali: I thought you were coming over tonight.

Cole: Open the door.

Open the... What?

It's then that I hear a knock on my front door. I panic for a minute because it is only ten o'clock in the morning and I am still sitting here in my sleep shorts and tank top.

"Angel eyes! Open the door!" Cole shouts as he knocks louder, sounding impatient.

I will probably regret this, but I decide it doesn't matter what I'm wearing, and I go over to open the door.

His mouth falls open when he sees me. He rushes inside, slamming my door behind us with his foot as he scoops me up in his arms and pins me against the wall. I have no choice but to wrap my legs around him as he kisses me senselessly.

We spent a good amount of time exploring each other's mouths over the past week, but that's as far as he would go. This is so much more, and I am loving it. He is almost manic in his movements, doing everything he can to get as close to me as possible.

He rocks into me, rubbing his hardness against my core and I feel like I am about to burst into flames.

His lips leave my mouth as he moves to my neck, biting and licking his way down until he is resting his forehead on my shoulder.

"Fuck, angel eyes. I can't believe you answered the door looking like this," he says.

"This is what I sleep in, and I wasn't expecting company. You act like I didn't know it was you!"

He pulls back to look at me and he looks almost pained. "You have no idea how sexy you are, do you?"

Me? Sexy?

"Yes. You are so fucking sexy. All you have to do is breathe and I get hard."

He leans in to kiss me again. This one is less rushed but even more intense than the last. The way his tongue pushes against mine with such force is turning my brain to complete mush. Between that and him sucking on my tongue, I am about to melt in his arms.

"Tell me to stop," he says between kisses. "Tell me to put you down and walk away or I won't be able to. I can't think with you in my arms, rubbing against me like this." His voice is strained and filled with anguish, but he sounds like he is enjoying every minute of it.

I hesitate to say anything, not sure how far I want this to go. I always pictured my first time being with someone I love, but lately, I can only imagine being with Cole. The feelings that I have for him are so much more than anything I have ever experienced. He is always on my mind. When I am awake, in my dreams, he is there.

If this isn't love, I don't know what is.

"Don't stop, Cole. I just... I can't... I'm not..." I say but am unable to express what is in my heart.

He pulls back to look at me. "Tell me, Ali. Tell me what's in here," he says, placing his hand over my heart. I know he can feel how hard it is pounding. My entire body feels like it is vibrating.

I place my hand over his and just hold him there. There is a short circuit somewhere between my brain and my mouth because I can't speak, not with how he is affecting me.

"What if I tell you what's in my heart?" he asks.

I'm not sure I am ready to hear it, but I nod if only to buy myself some more time.

He leans in and kisses me briefly before he shatters what is left of the walls around my heart. "I am falling in love with you, Ali. No, fuck that, I'm already there. I know it's fast and crazy and probably too much for you right now, but I'm just being honest. You don't have to say it back, but I wanted you to know where I'm at. There are no words that could possibly describe just how happy I am when I'm with you. My heart physically hurts when I have to leave you. This past week has meant the world to me. Just being with you, spending time with you, has been more than I could have ever hoped for. I know it's going to take you some time to get where I am, and that's fine. I'm not going anywhere."

I push back from him and slide my feet to the floor. I can see the hurt in his eyes, but it quickly disappears as I take his hand and lead him to my bedroom.

"Just go slow, okay?"

"I will take such good care of you, Ali. I promise," he says.

I thought I would be more nervous, but there is a calmness that washes over me. I know in my heart that Cole will be gentle. Hearing him say he loves me is everything, and I want to say it back but am completely overwhelmed with what is about to happen. Overwhelmed in the most amazing way.

He pulls his shirt over his head and my mouth falls open. His body is a work of art. He's fit, but not overly muscular. He's hard in all the places I am soft. There is a light dusting of blonde hair on his chest, and I reach out to run my fingers through it, eliciting a groan from Cole. He exudes strength, from his body to his personality to his heart. There's no wondering why I have fallen for him so quickly.

Once his shirt is tossed behind him, he drops his pants, leaving him in only his boxer briefs, which leave nothing to the imagination. His hands are clenched into fists at his side, and I know it is because he is trying to allow me time to become comfortable with this before he takes me. There is a slight tremor radiating throughout his body, and it makes me feel like the most desirable woman in the world to set such a powerful man on edge.

He allows me a moment to take him in before he steps into me and slides his hands under my tank top. His fingers slide up my skin, leaving goosebumps in their wake, as he lifts the garment from me. My hands immediately go to cover myself, but he catches them, holding them at my sides as he takes it all in.

"My god, Ali. You are so beautiful."

I blush, and with my top off, he can see just how far that blush runs down my body.

He drops to his knees in front of me and hooks his fingers in the waistband of my shorts. He doesn't pull them down immediately because he leans forward, and places open-mouthed kisses along my stomach. In this position, it puts him at eye level with my chest. He must realize this at the same time as me because he abandons his grip on my shorts and moves his hands to cup my breasts. He massages them gently as he leans forward and takes one nipple in his mouth as he pinches the other between his fingers. My head drops back, and I let out a whimper.

He pulls back immediately. "Are you okay?"

I grab his hair and guide his mouth back to where he was without a word, and he chuckles. Thankfully, he doesn't need any further invitation. He resumes his position, driving me crazy with his lips.

After a few pleasure-filled minutes, he moves his grip back to my shorts. He pulls them and my underwear down slowly, his mouth following.

He helps me step out of the garments and gently guides me back until I am sitting on my bed. His warm palm lands on my chest and he pushes me to lay back, all while kissing every inch of skin he can reach. I can feel his breath on my skin as he licks his way up my thigh. My fists are clenching the sheets beneath me when he finally makes it to my center.

There is a moment when our eyes meet. He holds my gaze as he leans in and tastes me for the first time. I don't know who groans louder, but I know that the fact that he is staring at me as he works takes this to an entirely new level. I want to squeeze my eyes closed so that I can focus on what he is doing to my body, but I can't break away from the intensity of his gaze.

I never expected it to feel this good, to be with another person. This is beyond anything I could have imagined, and we are just getting started.

I have no idea what else he has in store for me, but I can't wait to find out.

Cole

She's the one.

There is no doubt about it.

I love this woman with every part of me. I knew that going into this, which is why I think this is so much more intense than I ever thought it would be. I knew I wanted to wait until I was in love to have sex, but actually experiencing this with the woman that I now know I want to be with for the rest of my life makes it that much sweeter. I don't care what that says about me.

Hearing her moaning as I work her over makes me want to spend every moment of my life pleasuring her. There is something so empowering knowing that I am the one making her feel this good.

Her hands are in my hair, tugging and pulling as she thrusts herself closer to my hungry mouth.

"Cole! Yes!" she calls out, and it only makes me move faster and harder.

She explodes beneath me, and I can't wait any longer. While she is writhing through her orgasm, I rise to my feet and plunge into her warmth, thrusting to the hilt. We both cry out, and I try to think of anything else so that I don't embarrass myself by coming right away. She feels so goddamned good wrapped around me. She is hot and wet and so tight; it is squeezing me to the point where the pain and pleasure are mixing together.

Her eyes have closed, and I am immediately concerned that I took her too hard.

"Angel, give me those eyes. Tell me you are okay, please," I beg.

When they open, they are wet with unshed tears.

"Fuck, baby, did I hurt you? Are you in pain?"

A lone tear falls, and I lean forward to wipe it away. Just as I am about to pull out of her and beg forgiveness for being too rough, she says something that just about stops my heart.

"I love you, Cole. I'm not in pain, I'm perfect. This is perfect. Don't stop."

"Tell me again," I say as she pulses around me.

She blushes but smiles. "I love you."

I come down over her and rest my forehead against hers. We are breathing the same air that is overflowing with love. Nothing that I read in that book could have prepared me for the sensation of sharing this moment with the woman I love.

I take her lips, kissing her as I begin to thrust slowly into her.

"Fuck! It's so good," I say, pulling away.

My hands are planted next to her head as I pick up speed. I am trying not to be too rough, but it is so damned hard with how amazing this feels. She shocks me when she plants her feet on the bed and meets me thrust for thrust as she pushes against me.

"I love you, so much, Ali," I moan. "Come for me, baby. Come for me and let me know you're mine."

My voice is rough and filled with need as I try not to come. I want to make this good for her. I want her to remember this because I sure as hell know I will. This is something that will stay with me until we are old, and grey surrounded by our grandchildren.

A few blissful moments later, we come together, screaming each other's names.

Yeah, life doesn't get much better than this.

Chapter 11
Ali

Sunlight is shining through my blinds, casting a brilliant light on Cole's sleeping form. He has kept a tight hold on me for the past few hours since we passed out after our second bout of lovemaking.

That's what that was, right? We made love. I don't know if there is a difference between that and fucking, but it felt like more than just a release to me.

I have been awake for a while now, just watching him sleep. He looks so much younger like this, so relaxed.

It got really warm in here, probably because of how tightly we were wrapped around each other. The blankets have been kicked off, and his gloriously naked body is on display. I can't help but notice a very prominent part of him. Even in his sleep, he is impressive.

Without even thinking about it, I slide down the bed, getting closer to what I want. I keep checking his face to ensure that he is still asleep partly because I am a tad embarrassed at what I am about to do. I convince myself that I am only doing this out of curiosity, but that is a total lie. I want to feel him. Even more than that, I want to taste him.

I mean, it's only fair because he got to taste me.

I slowly reach out and wrap my fingers around him. My eyes are locked on his face but aside from a slight twitch of his brow, he doesn't move. When I am sure he is still out, I start stroking him. He groans, and his face tightens but he doesn't wake, so I take it even further.

I lean forward and lick up the entire length of him. He hardens and I can't resist putting him in my mouth. I wrap my lips around him and run my tongue along the tip.

"Fuuuuuck," he groans deeply, and I know he is awake, but I can't stop.

I slide my hand lower so that I can swallow more of his length. What I can't reach with my mouth, I work with my hand. His hands are now in my hair, guiding me up and down in a steady rhythm.

"Just like that, angel. Fuck, just like that," he says as he thrusts into my mouth.

I gag with how deep he goes, but I'm no quitter.

I have no idea what I am doing, so I just do what feels natural. By the sounds coming out of him, I think it is working.

The next thing I know, his hands reach down and grip my hips. He swings my lower half around so that my knees are on either side of his head and his tongue is on my core.

I hesitate for a second because I worry that I am smothering him. There is a deep concern that he can't breathe, but that is quickly replaced with pure, unadulterated pleasure as he licks me as if his life depends on it.

He thrusts his tongue into me, and I pull him from my mouth because it is just too much.

"Yes, Cole," I say as I rock against his mouth. His hand reaches down to grab his dick, holding it up for me in a silent plea. I know what he wants, and I am not going to deny him.

My mouth slides back over him and I take him as deep as I can, wanting to make this as good for him as I possibly can. His hands are now gripping my ass firmly, spreading me so wide.

I feel my climax building as Cole licks in between my folds. When he slides higher and sucks my clit into his mouth, I explode, screaming out his name.

"Fuck, baby. Turn around and ride me. Slide down over me, now," he says as he pushes me to move.

I can't get him inside me fast enough as I slam down on top of him. He grips my hips and helps me bounce up and down. The pace is fast but amazing.

"I can't hold off much longer, Ali. I need you to come," he says.

"I'm close, Cole. So close."

The air is filled with our panting as the temperature rises. He sits up abruptly and slams his mouth on mine as he thrusts up into me roughly. There is nothing smooth and gentle about it, but I don't care. It's what we both need right now as we desperately try to prove our love.

It only takes a few thrusts for us both to fall over the edge, coming together once again.

I collapse onto his chest, my head resting right over his racing heart. His fingertips glide up and down my back, sending chills down my spine.

"You know, for two virgins, we seem to be mastering this whole sex thing," he says into the quiet, causing me to giggle. Since he is still inside me, the motion causes us both to groan.

He flips me to my back and looms over me.

"You can wake me up like that anytime, angel eyes," he says as he leans down to kiss me.

"I didn't mean to wake you. I was just... uh... doing some research. For our project, of course," I say.

He chuckles. "Okay, well, you can research on me anytime."

I slap his chest lightly. I love this moment. It surprises me that I feel so comfortable with him. I think spending so much time with him this past week has helped me so much.

His smile falters, and I worry that I am crushing him. I try to climb off him, but he holds me tighter.

"Let me off, Cole, I'm hurting you," I say, but he won't release me.

"I'm fine, angel. More than fine, actually," he says. Once he is satisfied that I'm not going to move, he reaches up and cups my face. "I love you," he says, his voice firm.

I soften at his words. "I love you, too, Cole. So much."

He pulls me down and kisses me. It is deep and slow and full of so much emotion. He doesn't push for more, just slides his tongue against mine in a sensual dance.

When he pulls back, he rolls us to the side so that we are facing each other. I groan when he slips free, missing the contact immediately.

"Is this... too much for you? Did I take things too far?" he asks. There is fear in his eyes, and I know it is my fault. He is worried that I am going to panic and run from him. I don't blame him, but I feel guilty.

"Not at all, Cole. This was the best day of my life, and I hope we have so many more like it."

"I promise we will, Ali. But the day isn't over yet."

"Oh, yeah? What else do you have planned for me, tiger?"

"Tiger?" he teases, and I laugh.

"Yeah, tiger," I say with sass.

"Come over to my place tonight. Let me cook for you. The guys are all going out so we will have the place to ourselves."

His place? The fraternity? No way. I can't do that.

"Why don't we just stay here?" I say. I know he can hear the fear in my voice because his face softens.

"Angel, we can't hide away from the world forever," he says.

I know he's right, but it's too soon. I want to keep us safe and secure in our little bubble for as long as possible. "What does it matter where we are, as long as we are together," I say, but I quickly realize how that sounds.

"Exactly, Ali. It doesn't matter if we are here, or at my place, or somewhere else. I will be with you every step of the way. No one will hurt you. I won't allow it."

"I... don't know, Cole. I don't know if I can do it."

"Are you ashamed to be seen with me?" he asks.

"No! Not at all!"

"Then why? Do you not trust me?"

I push away from him and sit on the edge of the bed. My hands are shaking as the fear of the past threatens to consume me. I know I can't let it win, but it has been a constant battle within me. I wouldn't go anywhere with Laura for months after we met because I was terrified of what could happen. I wanted to believe she was genuine, that she was my friend, but I refused to let down my shields.

With Cole, it is so much more. I barely made it through what happened with Matt, and I didn't even really like him. I *love* Cole and I know that if something were to happen, it would destroy me.

He slides behind me and wraps me in his arms. "Sometimes the fear won't go away, Ali. The only thing you can do is face it. Face the fear, and just do it."

"I know," I whisper. "I don't know how."

"You can't let your fear of what could happen make nothing happen at all. It's one step at a time, with me."

He's right, again. I am letting fear rule my life. How much have I missed out on because of it, and how much longer will I let this go on? Cole's words make me realize that living in fear is a choice I don't want anymore. It's getting to the point where it could turn into regret.

I raise my trembling hands and place them over his arms and he pulls me even closer. My head falls back to rest on his shoulder, and he places sweet kisses along my temple and cheek.

"I won't let you fall, Ali. I promise. You mean too much to me," he says.

I turn and throw my arms around him. The tears that are falling are a mixture of joy and pain, fear and resolve. I never thought I would be able to open myself up to anyone ever again. It may seem silly to allow what happened to dictate my life, but it is something that I know will stay with me in some way, forever. There is still a part of me that sees myself as a fool for falling for it in the first place. I should have known I wasn't good enough. I should have realized just how much of an outcast I was. Then maybe none of that would have happened.

But Cole is different. He goes out of his way to show me my worth, to prove to me that I am beautiful. I know he would never do anything to hurt me.

"I trust you, Cole," I say into his shoulder.

I hope he realizes that to me, saying I trust him means just as much to me, if not more, than saying I love him.

Chapter 12
Cole

She trusts me. How is it possible that those words mean more to me than when she told me she loves me? Probably because I know how hard it was for her to say them.

I held her for a long time after that, whispering words of love and reassurance, trying to really make her understand just how much I absolutely adore her. Everything about her is so pure and innocent, and I will never take my new job of protecting her lightly.

I walk into my house and find several of the guys just lounging around. There are only six of us that live here full-time, but that means nothing. At any given time, there could be any number of people here just hanging out. The guys had been excited about a mixer at one of the sorority houses on campus tonight, so I really didn't expect anyone to be here. These guys are all about easy lays, and that is definitely what is expected of the mixers.

"What are you guys doing here? I thought you were all going to a party tonight," I say.

Trevor and Noah are playing a video game. "We are, but not until later. Why? You have a hot date or something?" Noah asks.

When I don't say anything, they pounce. "Dude are you finally going after that chick you've been pining over like a pussy?" one of the other guys, Hendricks, asks. He's one of those guys that insists on calling everyone by their last names. To be perfectly honest, I don't even remember his first name. He just moved in this year, but he's been a pain in the ass the entire time. I avoid him as much as possible because we just don't get along.

"Shut the fuck up. I need you guys to leave. I invited her over and I don't want you fuckers to mess this up for me," I say.

Trevor and Noah both know about Ali. They know she is extremely shy and nervous around people so they immediately climb to their feet. "Come on, guys. We can grab a pizza before the party."

"What's the matter, Buchanan? Afraid she might want one of us more? That why you want us to leave?" Hendricks taunts.

"Nah, not afraid of that at all. She's probably already heard about your microdick from all the other chicks you claim to have fucked," I say, and watch as his face turns red.

He charges at me but is stopped by Trevor and Noah. He's screaming and cursing at me, but I just laugh. This guy is a total prick, and I am done dealing with his shit. He is constantly running his mouth, bragging about how many girls he has fucked, and I'm starting to think he is completely full of shit. Whether they kick me out, or him, one of us has to go. I'm done.

Trevor and Noah are dragging him to the door when there is a knock.

Oh, please no. It can't be Ali. I promised her no one would be here.

I rush over to the door and pull it open only wide enough to step outside. She is standing there looking nervous as hell, so I pull her right into my arms.

I can still hear Hendricks mouthing off, so I know she can, too. "What's going on? Is everything okay?" she asks.

"Everything is fine. Change of plans. The party apparently isn't until later. Can we still go back to your place? I can cook for you there. We'll just have to stop and pick up some groceries on the way back."

"Uh, sure," she says, her gaze darting back and forth between the door and my face. I know she can tell something is wrong, but I just need to get her out of here before Hendricks says or does something to spook her.

To my complete horror, the front door opens, and none other than Hendricks is standing there.

He stares right at Ali and starts laughing. "Ali Eeeeew! Is that you? I wondered what happened to you after we graduated."

Oh, fuck no. This is the guy?

"You're the Matt that did that?" I yell.

All the color has drained from Ali's face as she realizes she is staring right at the past. She takes a few steps backward.

"Oh, this is rich! Buchanan, I had no idea this was the chick you were messing with! I would have told you how to ruin her even faster, so you didn't have to waste your time!" he says.

"Shut the fuck up, you piece of shit! You don't know what you are talking about," I scream, turning to face Ali.

She is shaking her head, back and forth slowly as if she is seeing me for the first time.

"Ali... angel... please. You know me. You know I would never do that to you! He's lying!"

"I thought..." she starts but stops. She looks like she is ready to vomit.

"Baby, please. Look at me. I love you. You know I love you. Please believe me," I beg, dropping to my knees in front of her.

"Dude, get up. She isn't worth it. I can get you much easier pussy than this chick," Hendricks says, and I snap.

I jump to my feet and tackle him to the ground, pounding my fists into his face. He is trying to fight back, but I have rage and love on my side. I need to avenge and protect my woman. I won't let this fucker's dirty words poison her any longer.

Blood explodes from his nose as I break it, but I am nowhere near satisfied. All I can see is the asshole who hurt Ali.

I'm not sure how much time passes before the guys pull me off him. Matt is laying in a bloody heap on the ground, crying like a baby, wailing loudly about his broken nose. There are threats of suing me and getting me arrested, but I couldn't give a rat's ass. All that matters is Ali.

I turn to find her, but she isn't there. I leap to my feet, frantically searching for her when I feel a hand on my shoulder.

"She took off, man. Right after you tackled him," Trevor says.

"Fuck!" I scream, allowing the anger to flow from my body. "I have to go find her!"

Trevor grabs me. "Wait, man. Think it through before you go tearing after her. She was in tears, seriously sobbing. Do you really think it is the right thing to do? She needs some space."

"You don't understand, T. She finally told me she trusts me, and this happens. If I *don't* go right now, what kind of message am I sending?"

"Shit. What are you going to say?"

"I have no idea. But I have to try. I love her, T. I love her more than anything and she's it for me. I don't know what I'll do if I lose her."

"I'm sorry," he says, but all I can do is nod.

Tears pool in my eyes as I think about what she is probably thinking. She must think I set this up. I had no idea who Hendricks was. If I did, I would have beat the shit out of him a long time ago.

My mind is lost, running through every possible scenario of how to get her back when Hendricks climbs shakily to his feet.

"You're the biggest pussy around, Buchanan! You have no idea who you messed with!"

"I know exactly whose ass I kicked, Hendricks. You hurt my woman. You destroyed her with your stupid, childish prank. You are the one who has no clue. Ali is the most amazing person. She is beautiful and kind and warm and caring, and I swear to all that is holy, if you ruined this for me, I will find you. The beating I just gave you will not even come close to the pain I will inflict on you if I can't get her back!"

"She's a nobody, man. She'll only drag you down!" he shouts but flinches when I run up to him and stop right in his face.

Even though I am filled with rage, I don't shout at him. No. Not this time. This time, I speak low, and even I am impressed with the menacing tone I manage to produce. "No, Matt. You are a nobody. You are a worthless piece of shit not even worthy of thinking of her. You don't deserve to breathe the same air as her. But go ahead. Try and go near her again. See what happens."

With that, I turn and walk away.

"Good luck, Cole. Let me know if I can do anything. I'm sure Laura will talk to her for you. I'll tell her everything," Noah says.

"Thanks."

I don't care how long it takes. I will prove myself to Ali if it's the last thing I do.

Chapter 13
Ali

I barely make it through my door before I collapse on the floor. I am tucked into the corner between the door and the closet, unable to carry myself any further. The pain is weighing me down, but I am not sure what is heavier – the embarrassment of falling for this again, or the agony of losing Cole.

There is a throbbing ache in my chest no matter how hard I rub.

I had no idea Matt was a student here. I had heard that he went somewhere up north, far away for basketball. Maybe he transferred. It doesn't matter. The only option I have at this point is to transfer myself. There is no way I would be able to finish out my last year at the same school as Matt... or Cole.

I can't believe he did this. I can't believe I trusted him. I feel like a fool, but even more than that, my heart has completely shattered into a million pieces, and I know there will be no putting it back together. Ever.

I jump at the frantic pounding on my door.

"Ali! Angel! Please, baby! I had no idea who he was. We only ever called each other by our last names. He just moved into the house this year. I would never do that to you! Please, you have to believe me."

Cole sounds completely devastated, but I don't care. He did this to me, to us. Anything we were building together has been destroyed.

"Please, baby. Please, Ali. I love you. Don't shut me out," he says pleadingly.

"Go away!" I shout but quickly cover my mouth. I didn't mean to say anything, I didn't want him to know I was here. It just slipped out. Knowing that he is right on the other side of this door makes all of this that much worse.

"Ali, listen to me. Listen to my voice. I didn't set you up. I didn't know it was him. If I had, I would have beaten his ass much sooner."

A sob escapes as I picture the way he charged at Matt and began pummeling his face. There was so much anger, so much rage. I would have never thought him capable of such violence, and it scared me. It's not that I thought he would physically hurt me, it was more that it made me realize how little I know about him.

"Baby, please. I need to hold you. I am nothing without you."

I rise to my feet, needing to get away from him. "Just leave me alone, Cole. It's over."

It pains me to do it, but I walk away. He continues to pound on my door and scream apologies as I move into my room and shut the door. I am about to climb into my bed, but stop, unable to lie down in the place where I confessed my love to him. Where I told him I trusted him. It was only one day, a few hours, in which I opened myself up to him, but it was enough.

I instead opt to climb into my shower, curling up in the corner. I shut the curtain for good measure as if it could protect me from the hurt.

What happened in high school seems like nothing compared to what I experienced today. To have the person I had given my heart to be the one to cause the pain is unbearable. In a matter of seconds, the trust that had developed between us was annihilated. I feel like I am drowning, like the trust that I had freely given earlier is now the water filling my lungs.

There is an immense sense of betrayal. But the most agonizing pain stems from the crumbling foundation of what I thought we were building.

My phone has been buzzing and ringing incessantly since I came home. I don't even want to look. I'm sure it is messages and phone calls from Cole, pleading with me to hear him out. But there's no use. I don't know that I could ever trust him again.

⎯⎯ ⟲ ⎯⎯

It has been days since I last saw Cole, not that there's any chance of me seeing him if I don't leave my apartment.

And I haven't. I can't.

I skipped all my classes for the past three days, not wanting to face anyone. I emailed each of my professors and claimed a family emergency. Thankfully, my lie was easily believed since I have never missed a single class before. I'm still doing the work, just submitting everything virtually.

Cole spends hours each day outside of my door. He is no longer pounding and screaming. It has changed into light knocks and soft begging. I had to turn my phone off because of how much he was calling. There were over a hundred text messages when I finally shut it down. I didn't read any of them because I already know what they will say. I just don't want to hear it or read it.

I have slowly been packing up what I can. I don't have a lot of boxes, but I have managed to use what I have to get as much done as possible. I spoke to my advisor yesterday, explaining that I would like to transfer. Since this year is almost over, I agreed to finish my classes this term and start fresh next year. I have applications in at a few other colleges and I am just waiting to hear back so I can decide where I am going to go. I can't really look for a new place to live until I know where I am going.

My parents are not happy with me, but they are doing what they can to help. My mom knows something happened, but my lips are sealed. I am not ready to talk about it to anyone. I'm sure she has her assumptions, but that will just have to suffice.

"Ali, please, baby. I just need to know you're okay. Give me something, anything."

Cole has been out there for the past hour. I am doing my best to ignore him, but it is tearing me up inside. I can't eat anymore. I definitely can't sleep. I tried playing music at one point to drown him out, but it only made him shout louder. I think he realized he was getting to me and started trying harder.

Every time he tells me he loves me is like another knife to the chest.

A commotion in the hallway has me going over to the peephole to see what is going on.

"You need to leave," Laura says angrily, shoving Cole in the chest.

"I can't, Laura. I can't leave her," Cole says weakly.

"Come on, man. Let's let the girls talk," Noah says as he tugs on Cole's arm.

"Move, you big lug. You've tortured her enough. Let me work my magic," Laura says. I have to fight the giggle at tiny Laura trying to push muscular Cole around.

"Ali, baby, I'll be back," he says into my door.

"Yeah, yeah. Get out of here," Laura says as she steps up to my door.

I pull it open just enough for her to slide in. I try to close it before Cole can see me, but at the last second, we lock eyes. His widen for a split second before they soften as he drinks me in. He fights against the hold Noah has on him, but I slam the door closed.

Just that one look has me melting, and I hate it.

"You turned off your phone," Laura says. Her tone is full of accusations.

"I had to," I say. "He wouldn't stop, and I couldn't think."

"He didn't set you up, Ali. You have to know that," she says. Leave it to Laura to cut right to the chase.

"Do I?"

"Yes, you do. Cole is not Matt. They couldn't be more different if they tried."

I turn from her and go back over to my packing. I have been working in my kitchen today.

"What are you doing, Ali? You can't run for the rest of your life. You can't keep pushing people away," she says as she comes to stand next to me. She takes the plates from my hand and sets them on the counter. "That's a lonely way to live, and you deserve so much more."

"If I don't let anyone in, I can't get hurt," I say weakly. I know it is a pathetic excuse, but it's all I've got.

She tries a different tactic. "Do you know why Matt transferred here?"

The sound of his name makes me cringe, and Laura sees it. I shake my head no. I don't really want to know, but I know nothing I can say will stop her from telling me.

"He got in trouble at his last school. The charge was harassment, but it was more than that. He hurt someone. Was close to raping a girl when someone stopped him. His dad apparently was able to throw enough money at the university to keep it quiet. They settled on him leaving the school."

"He hurt someone?"

She nods. "She's having a hard time from what I heard. Going to therapy and whatnot, trying to move on with her life."

I shake my head. What is wrong with him? What kind of person do you have to be to do something like that?

"Did you hear what I said, Ali? She talking to someone about it."

"You think I need therapy?" I ask incredulously.

"I didn't say that. I'm saying that she is leaning on people to help her through what she went through."

"So, what," I say.

"So..." she says as she slams her hand on my counter. "So what? That's all you have to say? I'm sorry, Ali, but you are wrong here. You are so wrong. I'm sorry for what you went through, I really am, but isolating yourself and pushing everyone away is not going to make anything better. Getting hurt is part of life. It happens. But the only thing that matters is that you get up, dust yourself off, and find your way back. You are so much stronger than you think, Ali. You let me in. Why is Cole any different?"

"Because I love him," I say.

"Oh, honey. He loves you, too. Can't you see it?"

I shake my head.

"Ali, he slept outside your apartment the first night. He would have last night if Noah and I hadn't come and dragged him away. He hasn't eaten, he hasn't gone to any of his classes. He is broken, Ali."

I slump down onto my sofa and curl up in a ball. "What do I do, Laura?"

She sits next to me and pulls me into her arms. As much as I appreciate the comfort, all it does is make me long for another set of arms; arms that I pushed away.

"I think you know what you have to do. I know it's not easy, Ali, but you have to let him in. That man is head over ass in love with you. I wouldn't lie to you. You know you can trust me, right?"

I nod, unable to find any words. The last time I said the words it was to Cole, and then everything went to shit.

"Talk to him, Ali. Don't let him slip away."

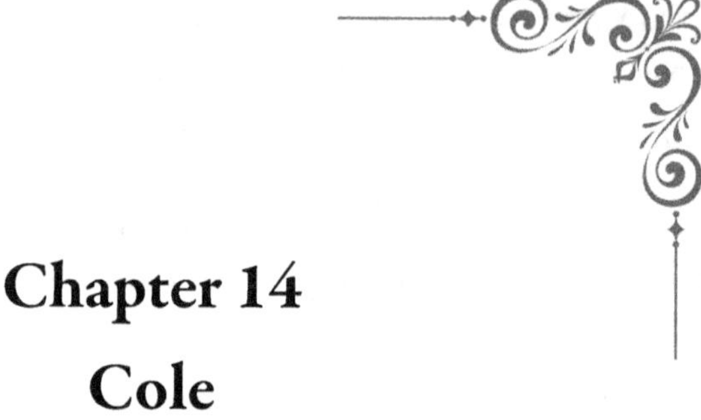

Chapter 14
Cole

I am not sure how I have any hair left on my head. The only thing I have done the past few days is pull on it. I needed the pain to prove to myself that I am still alive.

"You look like shit," Trevor says.

After Noah all but dragged me away from Ali's apartment, the three of us have been sitting around our living room. They bought some pizza, but I can't eat.

"I feel even worse," I say as I throw the slice that I had been holding back into the box.

"Laura is doing everything she can, man. You know we are all on your side here," Noah says.

"I know, and I appreciate it."

Silence falls between us, neither of them knowing what to say to me. I am losing my mind here. The fact that she is in pain, that she is hurting kills me. I can almost feel her agony like we are connected on some ethereal level.

My palm absently rubs my chest, but no matter how hard I press, it doesn't help ease the hurt.

I fall forward, my elbows on my knees, my fists in my hair yet again.

"Matt is gone," Noah says. I'm sure he's trying to distract me, but it doesn't work. I couldn't give two shits about what happened to Matt.

"Do you want to know what happened?" Trevor asks, and I just grunt.

"He called the cops to press charges against you. When they showed up, they asked us what happened, and we told them what he did. Turns out, he is already facing rape charges. Apparently, he forced himself on a freshman last weekend at the Sigma Delta party. So, when the cops heard about the commotion he caused at the house, they took him in. I heard a few others have come forward since he was arrested. His future is not looking too good right now."

"Shit. I'm glad I kicked his ass. He deserves it. Well, that and so much more," I say.

"What are you going to do?" Trevor asks.

"I wish I knew. She won't talk to me. How can I prove myself to her if she won't even listen?" I ask.

Noah smiles. "Grand gesture, man. You've got to come up with the grand gesture of all grand gestures."

Trevor and I exchange glances. "What the fuck are you talking about?"

"Listen. My girl reads a lot of romance books. I mean, a shit ton of them. She may or may not have talked me into reading a few. I can neither confirm nor deny it, so don't ask. Either way, in romance books, it almost always comes down to the guy having to do some big thing to prove to the girl how much he loves her."

Trevor laughs a full-on belly laugh. "You are so pussy whipped, man, it isn't even funny."

"Yeah, well, who's the one who will get his dick stroked tonight? Huh? I know for damn sure it isn't you," Noah says to Trevor, and now it's my turn to laugh.

Trevor's smile falls and he tosses a pillow at Noah. "Fuck you."

As they go back and forth, something hits me. It's like a hammer to the head and I jump to my feet, drawing both of the guys' attention.

"What is it?" Noah asks.

"I know what to do. I know exactly what I need to do," I say taking off toward my room.

I can hear them as I sprint up the stairs.

"I hope whatever it is, it works," Trevor says.

Me, too, man. Me, too.

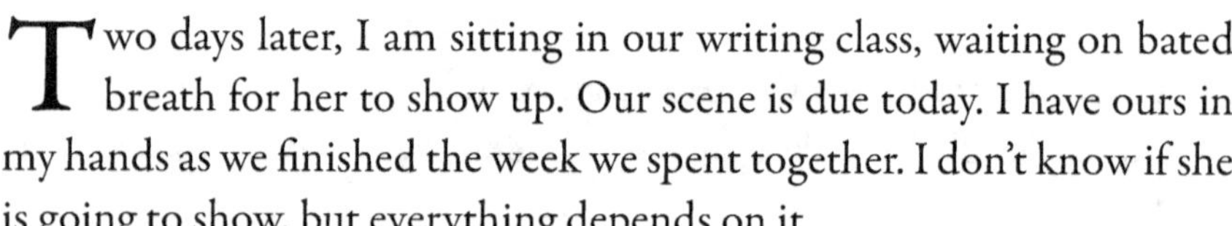

Two days later, I am sitting in our writing class, waiting on bated breath for her to show up. Our scene is due today. I have ours in my hands as we finished the week we spent together. I don't know if she is going to show, but everything depends on it.

Professor Marshall is greeting everyone as they enter. My eyes are glued to the doorway as my legs bounce rapidly under my desk. I spent the past few days working on my grand gesture, as Noah called it. I just hope I get the chance to set it in motion.

At the last second, I see her. Professor Marshall walks up to her and greets her. I can't tell what they are saying, but I do hear him ask her if everything is okay with her family. By the blush on her face, I can tell it has something to do with the reason she wasn't here the past two classes. He may not know her well enough to know that she was just caught in a lie, but I can, and it only makes me feel worse. She probably told him she had some kind of family thing to deal with to get away with not being here, but we both know it was more so that she didn't have to see me.

I don't dare blink as she makes her way to her seat. Her normal seat is a few in front of me, in the perfect place for me to watch her every move. She makes it a point to not look at me, but that's okay – in a few minutes, she won't have a choice.

"I hope you all enjoyed working on your scenes together. I am anxious to read what you have come up with. I know many of you had to step far outside your comfort zones on this project, but that was the point. I wanted you to reach deep down inside yourselves, to explore the creative part of your brain that you haven't used before."

Ali's fingers are toying with her notepad, tearing bits and pieces off to shred them on her desk. She is nervous, but even more than that, she is terrified. Her back is ramrod straight and her shoulders tense. I can only imagine what is going through her head right now. I would like to hope that deep down inside she knows that I had nothing to do with what happened, but her past is controlling her mind. One of the hardest things to do is fight against an invisible enemy. Mine just happens to be one of her memories.

"Now, before we proceed, I had an unusual request today. One of your classmates has asked to read a portion of their scene to the class. While that wasn't part of the project, and as I explained to the student, this will have absolutely no impact on the pair's grade, I cannot deny someone the chance to share their work. I want you all to listen and provide feedback based on the expected criteria of the genre. I am not going to give you the genre ahead of time because I want you to listen objectively."

Professor Marshall nods at me and I stand, ready to get my girl back.

As I move to the front of the room, Ali keeps her gaze forward. There are murmurs and whispers as I stand directly in front of Ali's desk. She sits in the front thankfully. I thought about what I would do if she chose somewhere else to sit, and I know I would have just stood wherever she was.

She still won't meet my eyes, but I begin.

She is about to get hit full force by my grand gesture.

Chapter 15
Ali

What is he doing? This wasn't part of the plan. I know Professor Marshall said this wouldn't affect our grade, but I swear if he ruins this for me... I can't even finish that thought because we both know I won't do anything. I'm too much of a wuss.

"So, Ali and I had to write a scene together, and we did. But I made a few adjustments without her knowing, so if you have any comments, direct them to me, because she had nothing to do with what you are about to hear," Cole says as he lifts the pages in his hands.

I have to sit on my hands because of how badly they are shaking.

"I call this scene "When Eyes Meet." I hope you enjoy it," he says as he stares directly at me. The room falls silent as my peers prepare to hear whatever it is that Cole is about to read, but the only thing I can focus on is the exhaustion on his face. There are dark circles under his eyes, his hair is frazzled and sticking up in all directions. On anyone else, it would look disheveled, but it just makes him look that much more endearing.

The second he begins reading, everything disappears but him.

"I remember the moment I first saw her. She was walking down the stone path, her chin tucked firmly to her chest, her body tight with tension. She appeared as if she was trying to disappear, to hide from the world. Her dark grey leggings molded perfectly to her legs, and she was sporting a white hoodie with our school's logo emblazoned on the

76

front. Her golden-brown hair reflected in the little bits of sunlight as it bounced and swayed with each of her steps.

I had no choice; her presence demanded my attention and I yearned to see her face. She had no idea how many people looked her way. Her sheer beauty was like a beacon of light on an otherwise dreary day. An overcast sky loomed overhead, doing what it could to darken the mood, but it had no chance against the brightness that she exuded.

Luck was on my side that day because she stopped, not ten feet from the bench where I sat. I didn't dare blink, afraid to miss anything about her as she reached into her bag. She pulled a ringing phone out and raised it to her ear. The movement made her raise her face up, giving me exactly what I wanted."

I can't breathe as I listen to Cole. He alternates between reading his words and staring deep into my eyes. I don't dare hope that he is speaking of the first time he saw me, but for some reason, I know that is exactly what is happening.

"When she said hello, two things happened. First, my heart stopped. Just hearing her say that one word set my soul on fire. The melodic tone coupled with the hesitant, almost shyness that encompassed her made me want to stand and pull her into my arms. It was an internal struggle that was impossible to win.

The second thing that happened was I fell in love. Crazy and impulsive, I know, but unpreventable when faced with the angel in front of me."

Cole was no longer looking at his paper and he shocks me when he places them on my desk. His eyes are staring deep into mine, and I am unable to look away as he continues.

"I never believed in love at first sight. I was that guy who scoffed at the concept. But Cupid struck me with a direct hit that day. I didn't think I could feel any better than I had at that moment.

Until I did. When her gaze locked on mine, I was gone.

No one ever tells you what happens when you meet the eyes of the other half of your heart, but even if they had, I'm not sure I would have believed it.

When eyes meet, the world stills. When eyes meet, everything else fades away. When eyes meet, the rhythm of your heart changes to match the rhythm of theirs. When eyes meet, you finally understand the meaning of life. When eyes meet, you can see the future and everything you have ever wanted.

I watched her from afar for years, never able to build up the courage to speak to her. Fate, thankfully, had other plans, as we were eventually thrust into each other's paths. She intervened again, pairing us together, forcing us to face what she had in store for us."

To my utter surprise, Cole drops to his knees at my side and takes my hands as he continues.

"I never knew how incomplete my life was until I felt her in my arms. Loving her has been the most extreme privilege, and I can't wait to spend eternity proving it to her. Gaining her trust was more important than conquering her heart because it was what mattered most to her."

A lone tear trails down my cheek, and he reaches up to wipe it away. He cups my face, running his thumb back and forth in the slightest of touches as he finishes.

"Breaking that trust was beyond devastating." There is a hitch to his voice, and a few more tears slide down my face. "Not because I lost her, but because of the pain that it caused. Regret is a fate far worse than death, and it has a firm grip on my heart. The week that I had her was the best of my life, and if that is all I ever get with her, I will be thankful, because, for that short time, she was mine, and I will never forget. Her touch is everything, and her heart is the purest of all.

No matter what the future holds for us, one thing is certain. I will never love another, for she holds my heart. It was given to her freely and without caution and I don't want it back. I have learned that if you truly love someone, then the only thing you want for them is to be happy, even if it's not with you."

More tears are falling, but he stops each one. It is as if he is telling me that no matter what, he will catch me if I fall.

He scoots closer to me and rises up on his knees so that his eyes are in line with mine. This time, when he speaks, I can tell it is not part of his reading.

"I love you, angel eyes. And I am so sorry for what happened. I'm not sure if I deserve another chance, but if you'll have me, I won't let go this time. Not for anything."

The room has gone completely silent around us, and I forget that everyone is watching. But I don't think I care anymore.

My hands raise on their own and cup his cheeks. He shudders at my touch and closes his eyes, leaning into me.

"I love you, Cole," I say in the barest of whispers, afraid that if I say it too loudly, the entire world will collapse. This moment is so fragile yet so significant. I want to move forward and stop letting my past dictate my future.

When his eyes open, they shine brighter than the stars as he leans forward and presses his lips to mine.

I am faintly aware of cheering behind us as the entire room, including Professor Marshall, breaks out in applause.

Cole stands and pulls me into his arms, never breaking our kiss.

After a few moments, he pulls back but rests his forehead against mine.

"I love you, so damn much, my angel. Thank you. Thank you for giving me another chance. I won't let you down," he says. His lips brush against mine as he speaks, and I can't help but chase them.

"Well, I can happily say that I think Mr. Buchanan and Miss Ewing have learned a great deal about the romance genre. Wouldn't you agree?" Professor Marshall asks the class, and everyone laughs.

"Professor, if you don't mind, I need a few moments alone with Ali," Cole says.

"Of course, Mr. Buchanan. Just a few minutes, though. I'm sure the class would love to discuss your take on romance," he teases.

Cole takes my hand and leads me into the hallway. I figured we would just stop right by the door, but he continues a few doors down to an open classroom and tugs me inside.

Once the door is shut, he completely catches me off guard by picking me up and pushing me against the wall. My legs wrap around his waist as his lips descend on mine. The kiss is intense and filled with more emotion than I can describe. Our tongues converge, each of us desperate to erase the past few days.

He leans over and locks the door before he carries me to the back corner of the room, all without breaking the kiss.

"I can't wait, angel," he says against my mouth as he sets me down and makes quick work of removing my pants and underwear.

He picks me up as he works the button and zipper of his jeans, sliding them down to mid-thigh as he plunges into me.

His pace is fast and hard but exactly what we need.

"I love you, so fucking much, Ali," he growls into my mouth.

My hands are pulling at his hair, tugging harder and harder with each of his thrusts.

"Cole!" I say as my head drops back. I missed this, missed him so much. I didn't think I would ever get to experience this again. I had convinced myself that I would just have to live off of the memory for the rest of my life.

But what he wrote, what he said in class made me realize how wrong I was about him. He didn't set me up. Cole doesn't have it in him to do something like that. I think deep down I knew that, but it was too difficult to understand. I'm not sure that I will ever fully accept that this amazing man could love me. *Me*. I don't feel worthy of his love, but after today, I know that he won't give up on me. Ever.

"I love you, Cole. I'm sorry I did this to us," I say.

He stops moving to stare at me.

"No, Ali. No. You didn't do anything. You were hurting, and unsure, and what happened was just a terrible case of bad timing mixed with a heaping handful of pure assholishness."

"Assholishness? That's not even a word," I say with a giggle, which makes him groan.

He starts moving again, but it is much slower this time. "It is a word. I just invented it," he says with a smirk. "Angel, you're it for me. I need you to understand that. No matter what happens going forward, we face it together. I need you to promise me that we will work through everything together from now on."

"I promise, Cole."

His thrusting gets faster and faster until we both go over the edge together. He continues to hold me as we both come down. His arms are wrapped completely around me, encasing me in his warmth. His forehead is resting against mine as I play with the hair on the back of his head.

"This past week was hell, angel. Being that close to you and not being able to see you, or touch you was the worst form of torture," he says.

I try to speak, but he stops me with a kiss.

"I'm not trying to make you feel bad, Ali. I'm just trying to explain to you just how much you own me. There is no future for me without you. I wouldn't survive. That week we spent together, even before we made love for the first time, means more to me than anything I have ever experienced."

I don't say anything right away, because I know he won't want to hear what I have to say.

He nudges me with his nose. "What's going on inside that beautiful head, baby?"

"I... I'm terrified," I say in a whisper.

His smile falls. He glances behind him to find a chair and takes a step back to sit down. He is still inside me, but I am straddling his legs.

"Tell me," he says softly as his hands come up to my face.

"You could ruin me," I say and hold my fingers over his lips to stop his protest. "Let me finish, please."

He nods.

"I know you wouldn't, but you have no idea how hard it is for me to believe that. You are the most amazing man, Cole. You are so smart, and kind, and sweet, and loving, and unbelievably gorgeous. And I'm just me. Nothing, in my mind, makes me worthy of your love."

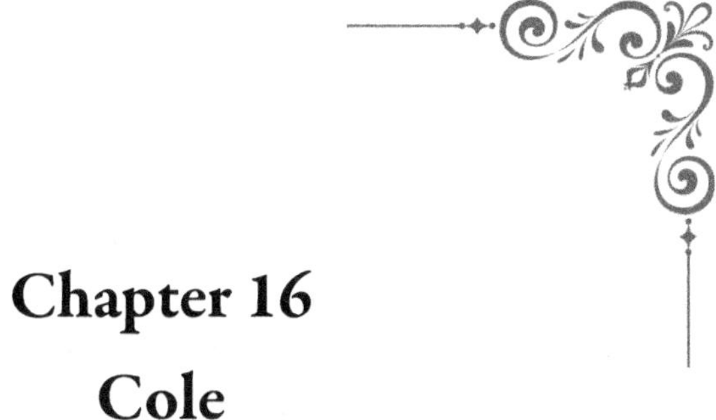

Chapter 16
Cole

I can't take the pain that I see in her face as her chin drops to her chest.

"Baby, look at me, please," I beg. This ends now.

I cup both of her cheeks and raise her face up so that I can look into her eyes.

"You have no idea, do you?"

"What?" she asks.

"I'm the one who isn't worthy of you, Ali girl. I know it is going to take you some time to understand that, but it's true. Everything I said in that classroom is real. That first time I saw you is etched permanently in my mind. I will never forget the feelings that coursed through me when our eyes met for the first time." I pause to kiss her, because, well, her warmth is still wrapped around my length, and she is just too damn beautiful. "You are beyond incredible, baby. You are who you are *despite* what that fucker did to you. He tried to break you. He tried to extinguish your light. But what you don't seem to realize is that he failed. Miserably. If anything, he made you shine brighter. You built walls around yourself, blocking everyone out. You made it almost impossible for people to see inside you. But, Ali, you don't need all that armor because what you have inside you... your strength, your beauty, your integrity, your compassion, your love... they can't break."

She throws her arms around me and pulls me into a kiss so deep and meaningful that it feels as if there is a direct line between her heart and mine.

I never knew love like this existed. I never understood that you could care so much for one person. I truly believe what I said, that without her, there is no me.

I can't wait to spend the rest of my life loving her, but I know that no matter how much time we are given, it won't ever be enough.

By the time we make it back to class, Professor Marshall is excusing everyone. Once everyone is gone, I go up and thank him.

"I appreciate you allowing me to speak today, sir. You have no idea how much it means to me," I say.

His eyes go back and forth between Ali and me and he smiles. "I'm glad it all worked out."

Ali blushes, and I pull her into me, wrapping my arm around her shoulder.

"I read your scene while you two were... out," he says with a smirk. He's no slouch, he knows what we were doing. "I think you should consider continuing the story. I think you have a great start here and would love to see more of it. Maybe even work in your little speech, Mr. Buchanan. I have to say, I think you had many of the women here today swooning."

"Ha!" I laugh, and Ali giggles.

"Well, they can swoon all they want. He's mine," she says quickly, then covers her mouth with her hand.

Professor Marshall laughs. "Well, either way, let me know if I can help. I write a little romance myself," he says.

The shock must be evident on my face because he smirks. "You should check out my latest book. It's called *When Eyes Meet*."

My chin almost hits the ground.

"What! You wrote that book? No. The author's name was something else. T. Marsh or something," I say in disbelief.

"A pen name, Mr. Buchanan. Just a pen name."

Ali giggles. Holy shit. I don't think I will ever look at him the same way again.

"Well, have a good day you two. Let me know if I can help in any way."

I lead Ali out of the room and outside.

"Did you know he wrote that book?" I ask.

She shakes her head. "No. I'm not sure if I would have read it had I known. There's something about reading sex scenes that needs to be anonymous." She shivers. "I don't think I will be reading anything else he has written. As good as it was, I don't want to picture him when I'm reading stuff like that."

I growl. "You'd better not be picturing anybody but me, baby."

She turns to face me fully. "Thank you, Cole. Thank you for not giving up on me."

"Never. I will never give up on *us*."

"Do you want to come back to my place?" she asks, and I nod eagerly. I know I was just inside her not too long ago, but after this past week from hell, I need more. So much more.

The walk back to her apartment can only be described as foreplay. My hand, which started at the small of her back, kept sliding lower. It may or may not have ended up down her pants a couple of times when no one was looking.

I'm not the only guilty one, though. She somehow managed to grip my cock a few times through my pants. She would stop to "point out" something to me, standing close so that she could guide my head in the right direction with one hand, while the other inconspicuously managed to stroke my length.

I groaned so loud one time that a passerby gave us a curious look. She thought that was hysterical.

So, by the time we make it to her door, I am all but groping her over her clothes.

"You are so going to get it," I warn as she opens the door.

I am about to grab her when I notice the boxes spread around her place.

"What the fuck? Are you moving?" I ask incredulously.

"Uh, well, I was going to," she says nervously.

Understanding hits me like a ton of bricks. "You were going to run," I say, the emotion gone from my voice.

She turns from me and moves over to the couch, patting the spot next to her.

I sit and try to pull her into my lap, but she shakes her head.

"No, Cole. I have to get this out."

I slide back, giving her some space, not sure I want to hear what she is about to say.

"I was going to leave. I put in some transfer applications to a few schools. I'm not sure where I was going to go, but I couldn't stay here."

"You wanted away from me that badly?"

"No! No, Cole. Not you. Him. Matt. I didn't want to be in a place where he could keep hurting me," she says. I get that. I do. But I can tell there is more. "But yes. I was running. From him. From you. From everything. I was taking the coward's way out."

I reach out and take her hand. "Is that what you want? You want to go somewhere else?"

"No. Yes. I don't know."

"Ok. Well, give me a list of where you applied so that I can get my applications going, too."

Her eyes widen. "What do you mean?"

"I'm coming with you. Where you go, I go."

"Cole," she says before she covers her mouth with one hand.

"Listen, Ali. I won't let you run anymore. But if you feel like you need a fresh start, I support you, one hundred percent. I don't care where I go to school, as long as I am with you. We can find a place together wherever we end up."

I can see her mind working hard as she tries to understand what I am saying.

"But, I do think you should know something," I say not sure if this is the right time to tell her, but she needs to hear it from me. "Matt was arrested."

"He was?"

"Yeah... for rape. He supposedly raped a couple of girls since he transferred here. So, between that and whatever he did to get himself expelled from his last school, he is facing some serious jail time."

"Wow."

"He won't bother you again, Ali. Even if he wasn't going to prison, I think the beating I gave him was enough to scare him away for good. I'm not sure what kind of dental plan they have in jail, but he is missing a few teeth," I say as I absently rub my knuckles. It hurt like hell when I was pummeling his face, but it was worth every bit of pain. Ali is worth everything.

Chapter 17

Ali

"Angel? You home?" Cole calls out as he enters the apartment. He is getting home from his last class of the day. Well, last class of college.

We ended up deciding to stay at Bane for our last year. We did move, though. He left the fraternity, and we found a small apartment together, far enough away from campus that made me feel like I was getting that fresh start I wanted.

"In here," I call out from the second bedroom that we converted into an office for us to write.

He stops in the doorway and leans against the frame, crossing his arms. I turn to face him and smile. His hair has gotten a bit longer, but I think he just enjoys it when I pull on it every time he is inside me.

"It's over. We did it," he says as he steps into the room and pulls me into his arms. I finished my last class earlier today.

We both applied for graduate school. We have applications out at several MFA programs across the country. Neither of us really cares where we go, it will just depend on which school accepts us both. Professor Marshall wrote us recommendations and we used bits of our first book that we wrote together as our submission sample.

Don't get me wrong. He still writes his sci-fi books, and I still write mystery, but we found that together, we are able to write some of the hottest romance stories. We ended up completing the one that we began in Professor Marshall's class. It is loosely based on how our relationship began. Marshall wanted us to submit it to his publisher, but we opted to self-publish. As much as we both want to be published, there was something more intimate about keeping this particular story small. It is so special to us, not only because it is our story, but because it is the first of many under our combined pen name A. C. Chanan. We thought it would be fitting to combine our initials with a shortened version of our last name. Well, my future last name.

Cole proposed a few months ago. Our first book has just come out, and we were opening the box that contained our author copies.

"Open it up. Let's see how it turned out," Cole said.

I picked it up, a chill racing down my spine at finally holding physical proof of our success in my hands. I flipped through the pages slowly, admiring the way the formatting turned out.

"What about the dedication page? I want to make sure it looks okay after all the trouble we had," Cole says.

"I'm sure it is fine. Just look at the rest! It looks amazing!"

"Can you just check, for me, please? I just want to see it," he said sounding nervous.

I rolled my eyes at him, wondering what he was so worried about.

I found the page and held it out to him. "See. Looks..." I trailed off at actually seeing it.

To the love of my life.
You are my heart, my everything.
Ali, will you marry me?

I was sure I was dreaming, but sure enough, when I turned to look at Cole, he was down on one knee holding up a ring.

"How does it feel to be an official college graduate, future Mrs. Buchanan?" Cole asks as he slips his tongue into my mouth.

"It feels pretty damn good, future husband."

Our wedding is scheduled for next month. We want to go off to graduate school as a married couple.

"I can't wait to marry you," he says into my mouth as he picks me up and pins me against the wall.

"Really? I'm starting to have second thoughts," I tease him, only because I love how dominant he becomes after I say it.

"Second thoughts, huh? Well, let me see if I can erase them," he says as he rips my shirt from my body.

As I stare into the eyes of the man I love more than my own life, I realize that Cole said it best that fateful day in Professor Marshall's class.

When eyes meet, you can see the future and everything you have ever wanted.

"I love you, Cole," I say softly.

He stills his movements so that he can cup my cheek. "And I love you, angel eyes. So much."

Yeah, life is good.

Don't miss out!

Visit the website below and you can sign up to receive emails whenever Michelle Rider publishes a new book. There's no charge and no obligation.

https://books2read.com/r/B-A-FDQW-ZLVEC

BOOKS 2 READ

Connecting independent readers to independent writers.

Did you love *When Eyes Meet*? Then you should read *Silent Hero*[1] by Wendy Zuccarello!

[2]

So, what happens when the person you are kind of stalking, ends up stalking you back, but you have no idea, so you keep stalking them? So, the stalker becomes the stalkee of her stalkee?It's not complicated at all.Casey Phillips is alone. She prefers it that way because if you are alone, no one can hurt you. At twenty-five years old, she has had enough people walk out of her life to know that she is meant to live a solitary existence. The only one she needs is her little chipmunk friend in her backyard. Well, that and her secret crush that she has been watching at the local park for the past few months. It's not really stalking because she is just watching him. Right?Dave Fredrickson can sense her when she is near. He knows she is watching him, and it doesn't

---

1. https://books2read.com/u/4X2RXv

2. https://books2read.com/u/4X2RXv

bother him one bit. But now that he knows she is there, he is overcome with the need to know more about her. He does his own stalking, but it backfires on him.When Dave and Casey finally meet face to face, there is an undeniable pull. But everything from Casey's past sends her running the other way.Can Dave convince her he is here to stay, or will Casey's demons prevent what could be a great future?Silent Hero is a standalone story with a guaranteed HEA and no cheating. You may recognize some friends from Michelle Rider's book, Above and Beyond, as Colby and Ember help their friend Dave find his forever.

Read more at https://www.wendyzuccauthor.com/.

Also by Michelle Rider

When Eyes Meet

Watch for more at https://www.authormichellerider.com/.

About the Author

Michelle Rider writes short, sweet, and spicy romance books. Come for the heat but stay for the love. Connect with me on Instagram and Twitter (authormrider) or Facebook (Michelle Rider). Email me at authormichellerider@gmail.com. www.michelleriderauthor.com

If you love romantic suspense or contemporary romance, check out my books under Wendy Zuccarello. www.wendyzuccauthor.com.

Read more at https://www.authormichellerider.com/.